Ready to rock. . .

. . .into Sadie Bird's strange world? Not only has she got to get her head around the fact that her brother is in the most embarrassing boy band in the world (their first single is so bad it practically makes Sadie's ears bleed), but she now has an unwanted room-mate. Who snores. And has multiple personalities, nearly all of them annoying.

As for playing referee in the Granny Wars . . . well, it's all brain-melting stuff. Thank goodness Sadie has two great best friends (even if they don't like each other) and her buddy Cormac to help her see the funny side of the madness. . .

Got to go; I feel *Sadie Rocks 4* coming on. Better get busy writing!

Mucho love

Karen McCombie

IT'S ALL GOOD
(IN YOUR DREAMS)

KAREN McCOMBIE

SCHOLASTIC

In memory of Jeannie,
the wrestling queen

First published in the UK in 2009 by Scholastic Children's Books
An imprint of Scholastic Ltd
Euston House, 24 Eversholt Street
London, NW1 1DB, UK
Registered office: Westfield Road, Southam, Warwickshire, CV47 0RA
SCHOLASTIC and associated logos are trademarks and/or registered
trademarks of Scholastic Inc.

ISBN 978 1407 10783 7

Typeset by M Rules
Printed in the UK by CPI Bookmarque, Croydon, Surrey
Papers used by Scholastic Children's Books are made from
wood grown in sustainable forests.

1 3 5 7 9 10 8 6 4 2

www.scholastic.co.uk/zone

Contents

Attack of the Nonnas

I sat in the graveyard, growling.

Don't panic; this isn't the start of some horror story. I hadn't turned from a pretty standard, slightly scruffy thirteen-year-old girl into North London's first ever genuine *werewolf*.

The graveyard just happens to back on to our garden (no, it's *not* spooky, it's *interesting*).

Actually, you can't really *see* the graveyard all that clearly from our house, 'cause of the small copse that I was currently hiding out in. ("Copse" as in small wood, not "*corpse*" as in dead body, in case you read that wrong.)

OK, back to the growling.

Suddenly aware that I was doing it, I stopped.

Leaning back against my pet Christmas tree – the one me, Sonny and Dad planted out here years ago, instead of dumping it with the rest of the post-festive-season rubbish – I took several deep, calming breaths.

In . . . and *out*. . .

In . . . and *out*. . .

In. . .

Thump, thump, thump.

I wasn't on my own. My growling and attempts at zen-ing out were being watched by two beady black eyes. Clyde, my slightly grumpy house rabbit, had hopped after me when I slouched out of the back door, walked the length of our slightly overgrown garden and wriggled through the bent metal railings at the bottom.

He stared up at me meaningfully, as he scratched at one furry ear with his big paddle of a foot (*thump, thump, thump*). Then – holding my gaze, like *that* would stop me from noticing what he was doing – Clyde began nibbling on the hem of my T-shirt.

"Oh, no, you don't!" I said, scooping him up for a restraining cuddle.

He'd done enough damage. I was already going half-blind after a week of trying to watch my favourite telly programmes on the Weetabix-sized portable from Mum's bedroom. (Clyde ate through the cable of the regular TV last Saturday night, *two* minutes from the end of the most exciting *Dr Who* EVER.)

So where was I exactly?

Well, trying to explain why I was so grumpy, of course. And I'll get to that in a second.

In the meantime, another question: what was I doing here, hunkered down in a copse on the edge of a graveyard?

The answer is, I was having some "me-time".

That's what it's called in fancy magazine articles, apparently.

In my *un*-fancy world, it's called getting away from annoying members of my family before I SCREAM. . .

Ah, thinks everyone. *You're talking about Sonny!*

Ah, *most* of the time, that would be the correct answer.

But nope, my irritatingly bouncy nerk of a twin brother was *not* the reason that I'd gritted my teeth ten minutes ago and slunk out of the back door before I exploded; he wasn't home from his school yet.

I mean, *yeah*, Sonny *had* annoyed me by staying in the shower for twenty whole minutes this morning, singing at the top of his voice so he couldn't hear me hissing that I needed the loo *now*.

And yes, I was *beyond* bored with how many times Sonny could drop into conversation the fact that the dumb junior boy band he was in was recording their first single in a few days' time. ("Mum! Have we got any honey? I need to have it in warm water for my throat, so my voice is OK for Monday"; "Gran – did you tidy away the lyrics for the song we're recording on Monday?"; "Dad! The recording studio we're at on Monday – did you know it's just along the road from your work?"; "Clyde – do you fancy doing some backing vocals at our recording session on Monday?" OK, so I *might* have made that last one up. . .)

I knew everyone (including my best mates Letitia and Hannah) thought I should be whoo-hoo-ing! at the idea of a member of my family having a record contract and putting out what might be a hit single. But honestly, you *had* to see how naff my brother and his bandmates looked (I mean, neon cycling shorts and matching baseball caps?!) and hear just how horribly cheesy their songs were to understand.

It's just . . . well . . . can you imagine the *shame* if his band ever made it and appeared on TV or in magazines? At school, I'd have to pretend that I wasn't really related to Sonny. *That* could work, since *I* went to a normal comp. in Highbury, and *Sonny* went to a fancy-pants stage school in Islington.

The drawback with that plan was a) Sonny and me unfortunately look a *lot* alike (skinny-ish; dark, floppy hair; matching moles on our upper lips), b) we both have the surname "Bird", which is pretty unusual and memorable, and c) his band is named after me: Sadie Rocks.

How flattering, if they were the new Nirvana.

How embarrassing, considering they were more like The Tweenies do pop. . .

But awful, awful, *awful* as that all was to think about, it wasn't the reason I'd been out here growling.

So who in my family was to blame?

To someone looking in, I guess it could've seemed like my mum, since she'd spent the last fifteen minutes bashing out an angry-sounding classical din on the piano (oh, for a mother who was a useful kind of teacher, like one who did cookery instead of music).

But nope, it wasn't her.

It could've been my baby sister, Martha, doing that high-pitched shrieking thing she sometimes does, where nothing helps cheer her up or distract her, and your head starts to melt with the noise.

No, it wasn't her either, not today.

It *could've* been my not-quite-stepdad, Will (he's not married to Mum, who in turn isn't *technically* divorced yet from Dad), who inevitably flips out when Martha does the high-pitched shrieking thing and says, "What's wrong with her? Is she ill? Is she just teething? Or should we phone the doctor? Or take her down to the hospital?! What's wrong with her? Is she ill? Or—" in an endless, panicky loop, till your head starts to melt with his infectious stress.

Nope, Will wasn't the guilty party.

I was out here after school this Friday afternoon, growling and trying to zen out, because of a relative who'd come to stay.

A relative who'd been here one whole day (and more importantly, one whole night) which had so far felt like a *year*. . .

"Guess what?" Mum had said brightly last Saturday morning, as she wandered into the living room after talking on the phone to someone or other.

I'd narrowed my eyes at her, spotting that her brightness was ultra fake. Mum really needed to take acting lessons at my brother's stage school if she wanted to be more convincing.

"What is it?" I'd asked her warily, as I sprawled on the sofa watching telly. (The big one; Clyde hadn't eaten through the cable at that point.)

Will was lying on the floor, jiggling Martha up

and down, observed by our cat (called Dog) from her prison cell (the large cage in the corner of the room that she was stuck in till her leg injury healed). Sonny was out at rehearsals (hey, did he *mention* his band was recording their first single on Monday?!?), so he wasn't here to find out, first-hand, whatever Mum's news happened to be. . .

"Nonna's coming!!" Mum had beamed, as if that was the most fantastic news in the world.

Her eyelid was flickering.

Last time it did that, she'd just caught eight-month-old Martha massaging a generous handful of banana porridge into the DVD player.

Anyway, back to the bad news. . .

Nonna was coming.

Nonna is Italian for grandmother, by the way. It might be reasonable and sensible to assume from that that my mum's mum is Italian, but uh-*uh* . . . that would be *way* too straightforward.

Need an explanation? Well, maybe I'll give you one later, but it probably won't make anything any clearer. Nothing is *ever* clear or reasonable or sensible with Nonna. . .

OK, I'll tell you this much: she started life as Muriel Bannister, then became Muriel Winters, then spent a few months as Mimi Rodriguez and is now known to all her friends and neighbours in

Spain as Bunny Humphries. Does that help? No, thought not. Told you.

Anyway, Nonna's got as many personalities as she has names. It's like having multiple grandmothers. At *least* six for the price of one. (What a bargain. . .) Off the top of my head, I could think of Funny Nonna, Nice Nonna, Generous Nonna, Tactless Nonna, Know-It-All Nonna and *Mad* Nonna.

"How long is she staying for?" I asked, noticing that Will had gone whiter than a pot of nappy-rash cream.

"Two weeks," said Mum, with a wide smile and the pinned eyes of a rabbit caught in the headlights. "She's having some building work done in her flat. So she thought it would be the perfect time for a visit!"

Being very polite, Will tried to hide his dread and ask a reasonable question. "And where is she going to sleep?"

Hurray for Will's question: I'd been just about to ask the same thing.

The *last* time Nonna visited us from Spain was three years ago, for me and Sonny's tenth birthday. She'd been especially keen to come and "cheer us all up", since Mum and Dad had just split up, and Dad had moved into the spare-room-cum-office above the garage.

The thing was, Nonna didn't *exactly* keep her side of the bargain. She might have been super-generous with our presents (there were a *lot* of Euros in our cards), but she cast a cloud of gloom over the whole visit. Like when Gran (our Irish, down-to-earth, mostly sane grandmother), appeared with a hand-made Scooby-Doo birthday cake for us, Nonna stole the show by starting to cry theatrically about the break-up, even though Mum and Dad were cool with it, and me and Sonny hardly *noticed* since Dad hadn't exactly moved to Bolivia or somewhere. (Through her tears, Nonna managed to annoy Gran by mistaking her iced-with-love Scooby-Doo for a *horse*. Gran got Nonna back by muttering something about how *she* was at least around enough to know what TV programmes her grandchildren watched. They *don't* get along.)

Apart from random outbursts of crying, the other drawback of that particular visit was that I'd had to share my room with Nonna. She kept me awake the whole night with snoring that was as loud as a road drill, but when I mentioned it (possibly rudely) the next morning, Nonna gave one of her musical laughs, as if that was simply the most ridiculous thing she'd ever heard.

"Sadie, darling," she'd said, holding me by the

chin and dipping her head to one side to stare into my eyes, "I've never snored a *day* in my life! And I've had three husbands, so I think *one* of them would have told me! You and your funny little dreams. . .!"

Well, at least I wasn't going to have to put up with Nonna's non-existent snoring *this* time round. With Dad in his new bachelor pad (the flat above the undertaker's on Blackstock Road), Sonny in *Dad's* old room, and me in *Sonny's* old bedroom, the reshuffle had left *my* old room free. It was destined to be Martha's and would be redecorated with gambolling lambs and fairy babies or whatever when she and her cot were ready to relocate from Mum and Will's room.

So last weekend, the decision was made – Nonna would have *my* bed, and I'd sleep on the blow-up mattress in my old room. I didn't mind – what was a lack of access to my wardrobe and computer compared to the road-drill torture?

Then, *WHOOSH!!*, the decision was suddenly *un*made, as the water tank above my old room burst with a flourish on Thursday morning, leaving one soggy mess of a carpet and walls dripping with damp.

"I'll be fine!" I'd said, standing in the doorway clutching my school rucksack, while Mum leafed through the Yellow Pages for an emergency plumber with the phone tucked under her chin. "Maybe I could just cover the floor in bin bags to keep me dry?!"

Outside I could hear Will start the car, ready to head to the airport and pick up Nonna.

"You have *got* to be joking, Sadie Bird!" said Gran, balancing Martha on her hip as she surveyed the damage. "You'd get double pneumonia by the weekend!! There's nothing for it. You'll just have to share with . . ."

The muscles in Gran's face tensed, as if the very thought of Nonna was leaving a bitter taste in her mouth.

". . . your *other* gran," she managed to mutter.

The thing was, I'd been willing to risk double pneumonia, even if I wasn't entirely sure what it involved, as long it stopped short of death. *Anything* but share with Nonna and her noisy nasal passages. . .

No such luck.

"Hey, I forgot Nonna could be so funny! Did you?" Sonny had said to me last night, as I rummaged in the bathroom cabinet for earplugs before I went to be tortured. I mean, went to *bed*.

"Nope," I said drily. Of *course* Nonna could be

funny (and nice and generous and tactless and know-it-all and *mad*).

Yesterday, once we'd both got home from school, me and Sonny had hugged Nonna hello, and she was – naturally – on her best behaviour. She'd been full of questions (a couple aimed at me, a million aimed at Sonny), and praise (specially for Sonny's sparkly talent), and dished out backdated pocket money to us both. And, of course, there were the funny stories of her friends back in Spain. I particularly liked the one about a couple called Janet and Norman, who were trying to organize an OAP flamenco troupe, made up of retired expats from Britain.

"So it's all good, yeah?" said Sonny over-optimistically, as he took the bundle of Euros that Nonna had given him out of his back pocket.

"Yeah, it's all good, in your *dreams*..." I mumbled, finding the earplugs and clattering the cabinet door shut.

"What do you mean?" asked Sonny, frowning my way as he let the sarcasm in my voice seep into his dopey head.

"We've had the *nice* version of Nonna tonight," I pointed out to him (not forgetting the funny one, *and* the generous one). "There're a *lot* more versions, remember!"

I nudged past him, determined to get to my room and get safely into a deep sleep before Nonna made her way up and started with the night-time road works.

Either Sonny was in denial or he had the two-second memory of a goldfish (possible), but he acted like he had no idea what I was on about.

In fact, he gave me a "See, she's fine! What's the problem?" shrug this morning over breakfast, after Nonna had praised Will's porridge and sung a bunch of Spanish nursery rhymes to Martha.

(Yep, more Nice Nonna.)

I didn't have the energy to shrug a "Wait and see!" back – I was too sleep-deprived (the earplugs hadn't helped too much).

But after school today, it started.

"You're really, really wonderful with Martha!" I heard Nice Nonna say to Will, when I came back in the door. Will swelled with pride. When Mum's maternity leave ended a couple of months ago, they'd decided that *she'd* go back to work ('cause she was head of the music department and earned more) and Will would give up his job as a PE teacher and be a stay-at-home dad.

"Now Will really *can't* be happy being a house husband! It's no job for a man! You'll have to give your job up, Nicola, and let Will get back to his teaching!" I heard Tactless Nonna say loudly to Mum when *she* got home from work. (Cue the furious classical music being bashed out on the piano just now. Guess it was a better, if noisier, option than bashing *Nonna*.)

And then my non-Italian grandmother turned to *me*. Uh-oh. I knew from the glint in her blue eyes that I was about to suffer from an attack of the Nonnas. I just didn't realize I was going to get all *six* in one blast.

"Ah, Sadie, come here and give your Nonna a cuddle-wuddle!" (Funny Nonna.) "You know, the older you get, the more you remind me of your poor granddad, lovely man that he was!" (Nice Nonna.) "It's just a pity that you and Sonny had to inherit that awful mole above your lip from him. And it looks so much *worse* on a girl!" (Tactless Nonna.)

"Um, I don't actually mind it. . ." I tried to say, gently extracting myself from her cuddle-wuddle now that I sensed danger.

"Now, let me take a look at it; hmm . . . you have to be careful; moles *can* become cancerous." (Know-It-All Nonna.) "Tell you what, for your sixteenth birthday, how about I pay for some laser treatment to get rid of it?!" (Generous and Mad Nonna, together in one short sentence. . .)

At that moment, I pretended I could hear my

mobile ringing, but the noise was actually just my brain jangling with rage.

So I left my many Nonnas behind in the living room, hurried passed Mum plonking angrily away on the piano in the hall, and took my non-cancerous mole (which I liked) and my jangling, rage-filled brain (which I didn't) out here to the copse for some fresh air and growling.

Sigh. . .

I had no room to escape to, thanks to the burst water tank.

I had no TV to speak of to take my mind off anything, since it was the size of a postage stamp.

And two weeks of Nonna was going to be more dangerous to my physical and mental health than double pneumonia ever could be (I think).

Bling-bling-bling-bling-bling-bling-bling-bling-bling!

The mobile in my back pocket genuinely burst into life.

"I've just arrived," said Hannah. "I'm in your hall – Will let me in. Where are you?"

"In hell," I growled, knowing things could only get worse.

Ripppp!! went my favourite jeans as I stood up and caught the back pocket on a branch.

See what I mean. . .?

Welcome to the bat cave

"What are you listening to?" I asked.

Letitia stood on my doorstep, blinking blankly at me. Maybe it would've been a good time for her to take the headphones out of her ears.

In lieu of an explanation, I reached over and held up her iPod, reading the info scrolled across the mini screen.

"No One's Gonna Love You" by Band of Horses.

I knew that track: ". . .like I do" – that's what the singer came out with after the title. It was a deliciously lovelorn song. All about unrequited lurve and all that stuff.

It was perfect for Letitia – lovelorn songs about unrequited lurve were all she ever had on her iPod. It helped her deal with the fact that her various Fantasy Boyfriends didn't know she existed.

Well, I guess maybe some of them knew she

existed (unless they were that Nickelodeon presenter she had a crush on a few months ago), but they certainly had no idea that she was hopelessly, tummy-churningly crazy about them.

In the past, her Fantasy Boyfriends had included the Nickelodeon guy, about a dozen lads at school (including Stefan Yates, who had the personality of an out-of-date can of tuna) and the boy who delivered her dad's *Sunday Mirror* newspaper every weekend. Oh, and I nearly forgot – she once tore a photo of a male model out of a *J17* annual from 2002 that belonged to her big sister, Kelise, and carried it in her purse till it disintegrated.

Her current Fantasy Boyfriend happened to be a pretty nice guy, and not likely to disintegrate anytime soon. That was the good news.

The *bad* news was that he was a seventeen-year-old trainee undertaker; but hey, you can't have everything.

"Who's here?" Letitia asked hopefully, finally unplugging herself and stepping inside.

"The Wizard of Oz. Who do you think?" I replied, turning to lead her inside.

I knew what Letitia was getting at. She was sort of hoping that Cormac (the trainee undertaker) might be visiting. Well, he *was* my friend (and Sonny's), but we knew him through Dad, since

Cormac's work (McConnell & Sons Funeral Directors) was directly *below* Dad's flat, and Cormac's flat (where he was temporarily living with his big brother, Kyle) was directly *above* Dad's place.

Dad and Cormac: they'd kind of fostered each other, I think. Dad missed me and Sonny endlessly hanging out with him in his old garage bachelor pad at home, listening to music and watching back-to-back comedy DVDs, and Cormac was happy to fill in for us. I guess Cormac missed squashy sofas and home comforts, while his parents' house was getting rebuilt: after all, Kyle's flat was a bit of a fashion statement crossed with the surreal set of a music video.

Anyway, the reality was, Letitia was more likely to bump into Cormac sitting on Dad's squeaky new black leather sofa, watching reruns of *The Office* with him, rather than here, helping Will change Martha's nappy. . .

"What happened to your jeans?" asked Letty, ignoring my amiable sarcasm and staring at my bum instead. Or at least at the torn section of denim that was revealing a patch of blue-and-white-striped pants rather nicely.

"Got mauled by a leopard. Got to change out of them. Coming up?"

"Sure . . . but *where is she?*"

Letty said the last bit in a hurried whisper. She was talking about Nonna, of course. Like Hannah, she'd never met her, and like Hannah, she'd come around for a bit of a nosey this Friday afternoon. And like Hannah, I don't think she could quite believe just how bad I said Nonna was.

"She's on the phone – hassling her builders."

I'd heard Nonna at it when I came in to get Hannah – shouting in Spanish for all she was worth. She was still going full tilt even now. It gave me a bad feeling; I mean, if *I* was the Spanish builder at the other end of that phone call, I'd be tempted to put my feet up and read the Spanish equivalent of the *Daily Mail* all day. I'd drag the job out for months on end while adding a couple of zeros on the end of the bill.

Help – what a thought! I mean, having Nonna here for a fortnight was going to be like an endurance test as it was. Any more than that and I'd be expecting our family to receive exceptional bravery medals in person from a member of the royal family who'd been dipped in gold for the occasion.

"Whoah!" muttered Letty, as she followed me into the room formerly known as mine. Not that you could tell; Nonna had made herself right at home, her two giant suitcases open and spilling out enough clothes for a year-long round-the-world trip. She'd also relegated my nail varnishes, hairbrush and tub of hairclips and bands to a corner of the dressing table so she could spread out her own array of lotions, potions, perfumes and giant pink foam rollers.

Not only that, she'd draped a dark-patterned silky scarf over the bedside lamp and pinned another bigger, red one – decorated with roses – at the window.

"Welcome to my cave," I said, sweeping my arm around to show off the gloom.

"Are there any bats in here?" joked Letty, stumbling up against my blow-up bed, unseen on the floor at her feet. It could have been worse; she could've tripped over Hannah, who was hunched on the floor counting how many pairs of shoes Nonna had laid out neatly in a line (nine).

Squeet!!

The blow-up bed made a dubious noise as I stepped on it to get to the window and hoist up the red veil to get some daylight into the room.

"It gives an 'ambivalent' feel to the room, according to Nonna," I explained, as my friends' puzzled faces came into sharper focus now that they didn't look like a pair of beetroots in a railway tunnel.

"Ambivalent . . . that means you've got mixed feelings about something, doesn't it?" Hannah asked, puzzled.

"Yep, but try telling Nonna that," I said, opening the window to get a bit of air in the bat cave. Anything to help keep me awake. "I think she really means 'ambient'. . ."

"Tell me again why you call her Nonna?" Hannah asked some more, straightening up from the floor and settling herself on the bed.

"When Mum told her she was pregnant, I think Nonna thought plain old 'Gran' or 'Nana' would make her sound too old," I shrugged. "So she checked out what kids in other European countries called *their* grandmothers, and thought 'Nonna' sounded the coolest, I guess."

Well, that was the *short* version.

For the longer version, we have to skip back thirteen years. That's when Muriel/Mimi/Bunny swooped into a hospital ward to visit her newly arrived grandchildren (yeah, me and whatshisname). Fresh off the plane from Spain, carrying armfuls of flamboyant flowers and gushing tears of happiness and doling out cheek-to-cheek-to-cheek kisses, Muriel/Mimi/Bunny breathlessly announced that she wanted her "adorable little angels" to know her as "Nonna".

"Isn't that just a *darling* name? It's Greek for 'grandma', you know!" she told Mum and Dad and a confused Gran, who was happy to be plain old Gran. (By the way, "nonna" wasn't Greek; like I said, it was Italian.)

Then Muriel/Mimi/Bunny/Nonna checked her watch and said she had to hurry – she'd got last-minute tickets to see a male-ballet-dancers-only version of *Swan Lake* at Sadler's Wells' Theatre.

Byeee!

She's been like that ever since, breezing in and out of our lives every couple of years or so, like a nicely tanned whirlwind.

And on that first-ever visit with us, she hadn't stayed *quite* long enough to find out that her adorable little angels had names. Not that she'd have approved, since neither "Sonny" or "Sadie" were on the suggestion list that she'd posted to Mum when she first found out she and Dad were expecting twins.

Thank goodness that back in leafy North London, my parents had the good sense to snigger at the list, then file it in the bin, or Sonny might've been Thor (Norse god of war) and *I* could've been Desdemona (from Shakespeare's *Hamlet*). Thor and Desdemona Bird . . . can you imagine? Urgh.

Oh, and before anyone who's super-smart

points out that Thor is actually the god of thunder and that Desdemona was in *Othello* and not *Hamlet*, I'd like to hold that up as evidence of Nonna's annoying habit of coming across as very worldly, knowledgeable and artistic, but of getting things ever-so-slightly *wrong*. And most infuriatingly, never *admitting* it.

"She's been married three times, y'know!" Letty told Hannah, glad, I think, to know marginally more than Hannah did about my family history. Letty and Hannah – they never miss an opportunity to get one over on each other. I like them both a lot, but I'd especially like it if they, er, liked each *other* a bit more.

"Who has she been married to?" Hannah asked me directly, without acknowledging Letty's intriguing snatch of information. "And what happened to them?"

"Well, Nonna was married to my granddad for years," I began, leaning on the window ledge. "But I never knew him because he died just before me and Sonny were born." (That was when she was Muriel Winters, wife of Bernie, housewife of Reigate, Surrey. She always describes my granddad as a fantastic man – the love of her life. Mum said they had separate bedrooms and hardly spoke to each other.)

"Then didn't she go to Spain for a holiday after

he died and end up marrying someone else after ten minutes?" Letty prompted me.

"Ten *days*," I corrected her. "That was Alejandro. She ate at his café every night. He was a widower, and she loved it when he gave her the nickname 'Mimi', because he found it too hard to say 'Muriel'."

"And that was enough to make her fall in love and marry him?" asked Hannah, aghast.

"Pretty much," I said, idly leaning over and plucking one of Nonna's pink foam rollers out of the netting bag she kept them in. I began experimentally rolling up a chunk of hair in it. "Then when she sussed out that he expected her to work in the café with him night and day, she fell *out* of love pretty quickly too. I never met him – she divorced him when me and Sonny were still little."

"And who came next?" asked Hannah, kicking off her trainers and slipping her feet into two gold sandals. She stuck her legs up in front of her to check out whether she suited glamorous shoes for the over-sixties.

Letty, meanwhile, had started to sniff at the bottles of lotions and potions.

"Well, she might not have liked being Mrs Rodriguez very much, but she loved Spain and decided to retire there. And then she met Jack Humphries. He was, like, a hundred and twelve or something," I said vaguely, hazily recollecting meeting a very old, bald man a few times when I was little and visiting Nonna in Spain. "He called her 'Bunny', and it sort of stuck. But he died when me and Sonny were about six, I think."

"What of?" asked Letty, taking a deep sniff from a tall, lemon-coloured bottle.

"Dunno," I muttered, trying to remember. "She talks a lot. Maybe he just needed a rest. . ."

Hannah and Letty both started giggling, which was nice, 'cause it gave the illusion that we were all friends together instead of separately.

"So whereabouts in Spain does your n –" Hannah seemed to struggle to say the unconventional name. "– I mean, your *gran* live?"

"Hello, hello! What's going on here – is my grandaughter boring you with my life story?"

Nonna stood in the doorway of the room, looking magnificent. Her skin was golden, her hair was silvery blonde and the huge, chunky moonstone pendant around her neck perfectly matched the blue-grey, silky, bat-wing cardie she was effortlessly wearing draped just off the shoulders of her white linen top.

Letitia didn't look particularly magnificent,

with the white lemony circle of body lotion ringing her nose.

She didn't know it was there, which made her less self-conscious than Hannah, who quickly lowered her feet, shuffling the gold shoes off and kicking them back underneath my bed.

"Nonna," I said hurriedly, to cover up from the shock of being caught gossiping, "these are my friends Letitia and Hannah."

"Lovely to meet you," smiled Nonna, holding her hand out graciously to first Letty and then Hannah. "Please call me Bunny; everyone does!"

Letty and Hannah smiled weakly. I just knew that the idea of calling a sixty-five-year-old woman "Bunny" was as weird to them as calling a passing policeman "sweetie-pie". It wasn't going to happen, I could tell.

"You know, in her phone calls, I've heard Sadie mention your names *so* often that I feel as if I know you already."

To be honest, I never really talked to Nonna for very long on the phone. I'd fill up conversations with tales of school, and of Letty and Hannah, and then tick-tock, tick-tock, count down the seconds till I knew she'd start asking about Sonny and how stage school was going. It would've been fair enough, except I knew it didn't happen in reverse.

(I'd secretly listened in to enough of Sonny and Nonna's calls to reassure myself that I wasn't just being paranoid. And I wasn't. The number of times my name cropped up was an unsurprising *zero*.)

Letty and Hannah stared at her, slightly hypnotized, as if some grand Hollywood dame had appeared in our tiny corner of North London.

"And Letitia is *such* a beautiful name," said Nice Nonna, kindly not mentioning the ring of nose cream. "It's popular in Spain too. Did you know it means . . . let me think now . . . I do *love* the meaning of names. Oh, yes! It means 'wildflower', I'm sure of it!!"

I bet it didn't.

I felt like getting online right now and checking that Nonna factlet out.

"Wow!" said Letitia, entranced.

"Do you know the meaning of mine?" asked Hannah, eagerly.

"Not off the top of my head, my love, but it might come to me."

Uh-oh. Nonna had cast her charm spell on them.

Poor Letty and Hannah. The disappointment – when she morphed into one of the other versions of Nonna – would come as quite a shock.

"Now, I heard one of you girls asking where in Spain I live. Well, it's the most *beautiful* cliff-top town, which was once an artists' colony."

Both my friends automatically formed their mouths into the shape of interested "o"s.

"It's spelt M-O-J-A-C-A-R, but you must pronounce it the proper Spanish way, which is '*Mo-ha-car*'. Can you try that for me?"

Oh, no. I mean, *please*.

I could see the interested "o"s on Letty and Hannah's mouths switching to tight-lipped awkwardness.

"Come *on*, girls! You first, Letitia, my little wildflower! '*Mo-ha-car*'!!"

"Uh . . . Mo-ha-car. . ." mumbled Letty, like she might just want to die.

"*Good* try! Now your turn, Hannah!! '*Mo-ha-car*'!"

I thought Hannah might just fake a faint to get out of the embarrassment, but she managed a whispered "Mo-ha-car".

"Sadie, now *your*—"

"Mo-ha-car," I said hurriedly, just to get it over with.

"Ha, ha, ha! Not a lot of expression there, Sadie, sweetheart! You certainly haven't inherited my theatrical gene – only Sonny got that!" said Nonna, tossing her sweep of silvery blonde hair back as she laughed.

"I guess," I mumbled, through gritted teeth.

"Oh!" Nonna jumped at the sound of the slammed front door and Sonny's boisterous hello. "There he is now! Sonny, honey! YOO-HOO!!"

And with a swoosh of her silky, bat-wing cardie, she was gone. Gone to hug that chip off the old block: my multi-talented brother.

"Uh, was your gran once an actress or something?" Letty frowned at me.

"Never," I replied. "She used to be a doctor's receptionist."

You know, when Nonna was a kid – back when she was Muriel Bannister – I bet her school reports said "*Muriel has a very vivid imagination*".

"She's kind of . . . *mad*!!" said Hannah, in obvious shock.

"I *told* you so," I said in a slightly superior tone – till I caught sight of myself in the mirror and realized I had a pink foam roller in my fringe.

"Can we go watch her some more?" asked Letitia, mesmerized by Nonna's nuttiness.

She was talking about my grandmother as if she was a bizarre animal in a zoo. Which suited her pretty well, come to think of it.

"Sure," I said. "Let's go watch her slobbering over Sonny."

The zoo thing; *there* was an idea. Maybe we could put Nonna in a cage same as the one Dog was stuck in, only bigger (well, wouldn't want to be cruel), and only feed her if she behaved herself.

It might be the only way to survive the next fortnight.

Other than that, I might have to hope I got struck down by a non-lethal illness that would put me in a relaxing, oblivious two-week coma. . .

To be continued. . .

"Letitia means 'joy'."

Cormac practically choked on his fried breakfast. My gran (the relatively sane Irish one) patted him on the back of his black funeral suit.

"Nothing to do with wildflowers, then?" he asked, once he'd caught his breath.

"Nope, and Hannah means 'gracious'," I told him. "I'm dying to hear what Nonna makes up for it, though. She'll probably say it's 'seagull' or something. . ."

"Did you check the name stuff on the internet, then?" asked Dad, grinning and rubbing his own tummy after second helpings of Gran's mega mid-morning breakfast.

It was Saturday, and since Dad's wholesale business (Bird's Paper Products) didn't generally open on Saturdays, he was taking it easy. The same couldn't be said for Cormac – death didn't take much notice of the weekend, and a recently bereaved someone-or-other was due downstairs at McConnell & Sons in about five minutes.

"Yep," I answered, helping myself to some scrambled egg and toast.

I'd checked online this morning. In the *loooonggg*, sleepless, snore-filled hours that I'd lain awake, I decided I'd get on the computer as soon as I got up.

"Sadie, darling . . . do you *have* to?" Nonna had mumbled from the bed in the red-gloomed bat cave, as I keyed Letitia's name into a search engine. "I've had the most *awful* night and hardly slept."

I wanted to say liar, liar, pants on fire, but it's not the sort of thing you say to your grandmother, even if you have a valid point.

"You know, I think I must be allergic to your pets," Nonna had mumbled, pulling her eyeshade back into place. "A house is no place for a rabbit – they cause *Lyme* disease, you know. I think I may have to have a lie-in. . ."

"Nonna's having a lie-in," I told Mum and Will once I'd trudged down the stairs.

I was sure I could see a look of relief on their faces.

But that was the thing; I could never talk to Mum about the general confusing, annoying nuttiness of Nonna. I was ninety per cent sure that Mum felt exactly the same as me – specially since she suffered from Attacks of the Nonnas too – but she didn't seem to be able to handle anyone criticizing her mother.

I guess that's a mum–kid thing. I mean, *my* mum can be a bit flaky too, specially when she's listening to classical music and ignoring what I'm saying – but I'd go in a complete huff with anyone who tried to call her flaky to my face.

As for Will? Well, Will always pretends everything's eternally "cool" (his catchphrase), even when it patently *isn't*, so even if Nonna was poking him with big, sharpened pointy sticks, I bet he'd keep smiling through gritted teeth and act like he was having a lot of fun.

And Sonny? Sonny was so self-absorbed on a daily basis that *plenty* of Nonna's nuttiness passed him by. Or he just conveniently forgot it as soon as Nonna started asking him – all starry-eyed – for the latest updates on his plans for superstardom.

Where was the Boy Wonder now? Off to rehearsals, as usual, getting his voice limbered up for recording his band's cheese-fest of a song in two days' time.

So what would I do with the unexpected peace and undisturbed quiet of this particular Saturday morning? Well, not watch the titchy telly, that was for sure. (Why start a day with a migraine?)

I can escape! I thought to myself, deciding that in the circumstances (i.e., Nonna was still sleeping), it wouldn't be rude to slope off to Dad's flat for a visit.

And now here I was – ten minutes' walk away – relaxing, entertaining Dad, Gran and Cormac with tales of Nonna, and finding out what I already suspected; i.e., that rabbits categorically *don't* cause Lyme disease (the less floppily cute and furless tick is responsible for that).

"Oh, and she said she'd pay for me to have my mole removed, since it might go septic or cancerous or something," I added, remembering another nugget.

Cormac was having serious trouble getting through his breakfast. He'd nearly sprayed orange juice out of his nose when I told him about Nonna trying to get me, Letitia and Hannah to all say "*Mo-ha-car*" in rotation, like we were five-year-olds learning the alphabet.

He was here, by the way, because my gran had taken pity on him. His brother, Kyle, was off on location for a few days, to some far-flung tropical destination, doing hair and make-up on a magazine fashion shoot. (What *would* the statuesque models make of the fact that he'd practised his skills by doing make-up on dead people? Faint from their grand, statuesque heights, probably.)

Anyway, Gran decided that Cormac would fade away from malnutrition if she didn't insist on him coming downstairs for meals. She seemed oblivious to the fact that his mum and dad were perfectly capable of feeding him when he popped home to their half-renovated house in just-along-the-road Stoke Newington for visits.

But then Gran did so *love* to be useful, and liked to think everyone was incapable of looking after themselves, so that she had a legitimate reason to help out. It's why she was constantly round at our place, lending a hand with Martha and not being able to stop herself from putting on a boil wash or trimming the shrubbery at the same time without being asked.

It was also why she'd "temporarily" moved in to Dad's shoebox-sized spare room here in the flat above the funeral parlour; to help him "settle in" after the "trauma" of finally moving out of the room above the garage at home, three years after he'd promised Mum he would.

"Oh, for the love of God!" Gran gasped, fanning herself with the tea towel in shock at what current nonsense Nonna had come out with. "Laser treatment indeed! On such a lovely beauty spot!! Honestly, that *woman*. . ."

I appreciated Gran's support, I really did. I knew that she'd been niggled by Nonna over the years; they were as different as chalk and chilli-flavoured cheese. Even when I was little, I could tell that Nonna patronized Gran (even if I didn't know what the word "patronized" meant) and spotted that Nonna was as interested in Gran as a drab potted plant (though Gran always got her own back with audible dark mutterings under her breath).

Still, I'd have appreciated it more if Gran had suddenly announced that she very much missed her tidy little bungalow in Barnet and could I give her a hand with the packing, as a taxi was arriving in ten minutes. Then I could've hopefully, maybe, possibly moved into the boxroom and become Dad's lodger for the duration of Nonna's trip.

"Ah . . . I remember the first time I met Muriel," said Dad, leaning back in his chair and grinning. Dad called Nonna "Muriel" behind her back, 'cause that was her name when he was introduced to her, and "Bunny" to her face since she insisted everyone did. "I thought I'd really won her over. When I was leaving, she gave me a kiss on the cheek and said, 'Martin, you're adorable! But then shorter men often *are*, to make up for their lack of height. . .'"

Gran *tsk*ed loudly and overlong, then stomped off to make herself useful in the tiny kitchen just off the living room.

"But . . . your name's *Max*!" said Cormac, frowning so much that his eyebrows nearly met in the middle. "'And you're not even particularly short!"

"Oh, don't expect sense when it's anything to do with Nonna!" I told him, taking a big bite of my toast.

"Wow . . . I'd love to meet her!" he said, his eyes lighting up. Yeah, lighting up 'cause he was suddenly inspired. Aside from learning the delicate art of undertaking, Cormac was also desperate to make it as a stand-up comedian, and had already put on a couple of "shows" in Highbury Fields, standing on a wooden crate in his stern black suit, trying out his routines on any random, passing Sunday-morning dog walkers (plus me, Dad, Sonny, Letty and Hannah).

I knew the stuff we were telling him about Nonna was going *straight* into a box in his head marked "Possible Comedy Material".

But as for him meeting Nonna – I wasn't so sure about that. He was tall and gangly, pale as milk with bright, fiery red hair and a mighty shy streak. Put that lot together with his weird job and weirder hobby, and the chances of Tactless, Know-It-All and Mad Nonnas keeping their tongues were non-existent. Thinking she was being particularly charming, Nonna would probably *annihilate* him.

"You'd need a force field around you just to deflect her comments!" Dad joked.

"That bad?!" laughed Cormac.

"*That* bad!" nodded Dad. "Sadie, for selflessly sharing a room with Nonna, I salute you! Though if *I* were you, I'd drag my blow-up bed through to Sonny's room."

"What?!" I half-coughed, half-shrieked. "At least Nonna stops talking, even if she snores. Sonny would never shut up. He'd completely do my head in!"

And at least I knew what was underneath *my* bed: a well-used game of Monopoly and an old pink suitcase full of ancient birthday cards.

The underneath of Sonny's bed was a fearsome, dark world, full of unknown items, some of which were obviously well-worn socks garnished with dust and fluff, and some of which were . . . well, who *knows*.

All I *did* know was that I'd never be able to sleep with all that ominous debris right at eye (and nose) level.

"Hey! I've just had an idea!" said Dad, suddenly clicking his fingers.

Dad's ideas were usually along the lines of "Hey! I've had an idea! Let's go to the City Farm and pet a pig!/mime along to every track on the Beatles' *Abbey Road*!/buy five trifle mixes and make a really *big* trifle!"

"Yeah?" I said, hopeful that maybe *this* time Dad's idea would be less on the goofy and more on the useful side. Something to do with Nonna, I hoped. Something that would help make her stay more bearable.

Please. . .

"Well, I was just thinking—"

Hold it!

I'm not going to spill Dad's idea yet. I'm going to let the tension mount, just like at the end of the first half of a double bill of *Dr Who*.

To Be Continued, it'd say.

So let's keep the suspense going. . .

Let the Granny Wars commence. . .

Despite the snoring onslaught, I must have slept a *bit* last night, 'cause I had a dream.

In the dream, Dad's idea turned out to be *humungous*.

He turned to me in a glow of light, the idea so dazzling that it gave him an aura of rainbow hues.

"Listen . . . *I'll* take a break from work, and I'll phone your school and get permission to take you out. For the next two weeks, we're going on holiday to Disney World Florida, where we'll go on ONLY the scariest rides, followed by a two-day trip to Graceland in Memphis, Tennessee, to see Elvis's grave!"

It was an amazing idea, and an amazing dream (apart from the bit about Elvis, as neither me nor Dad were particularly *into* Elvis Presley and his music – though since he'd moved out, Dad's sandy-coloured sideburns were growing worryingly long and Elvis-esque. Maybe they were psychologically damaging me and *that's* why they were invading my subconscious.)

Anyway, scary Elvis sideburns aside, the dream got better.

"Is Sonny coming too?" I asked, blinking at the radiant being who was my father.

"No – he'll be too busy doing his rubbish band stuff."

Told you it got better.

But I think even in my sleep, I became aware that I was only dreaming. Even though Dad thought boy bands in general were as fantastic as the bubonic plague, he was – like the rest of my family (except me) – deliriously excited for Sonny and his bid for fame.

By the way, I'd like to apologize right now for hyping up Dad's idea and all that suspense stuff.

It was dumb, and unforgivable, I know, but I was desperate, because Dad's *actual* idea was pants.

"OK, here it is . . ." Dad said in reality, with a tiny speck of tomato sauce at the corner of his mouth.

(There was no rainbow-coloured aura. Dad is just a paper-plate wholesaler, after all, and not a demigod.)

". . . you know I've got this new client?"

Yeah, I knew. Sort of. The client was the owner of a modern-but-retro-look restaurant that was opening near Highbury Corner. Dad was doing all their paper napkin and tablecloth requirements. I love my dad, but . . . *snore*.

"Uh-huh," I said with an unenthusiastic nod.

"Well, he invited me along to the opening night of his new restaurant tonight – said it would be a laugh," he chattered on. "But actually *now* I'm just thinking –"

Dad dropped his voice and glanced towards the kitchen, to make sure Gran wasn't about to pop out and hear what he was saying. The fool; didn't he *know* she'd be standing right at the door, polishing something up with the tea towel and earwigging?

"What?" I asked, attempting to egg him on.

"– I was thinking we should *all* go!" Dad whispered. "Me, you, Sonny, Mum, Will, Martha, Gran and Nonna. Great food . . . party atmosphere . . . might melt the frostiness between your Gran and Muriel. And give your mum a night off from having her cooking criticized!"

He had a point with the cooking thing. Nonna ate her tofu stir-fry last night like it was stir-fried sewage, then said she *must* give Mum her recipe for the most divine paella. ("It's pronounced 'pie-YAY-ya', you know," Nonna had said. I kind of hoped Mum would stick her fingers in her ears at that point and sing "La-la-LA!! Can't HEAR you!!" But sadly she didn't.)

Still, it was a *pants* idea. Being in a public place, Nonna would be worse than ever. The lesser-known Show-off Nonna (a close relative of Know-It-All Nonna) would be out in force, within seconds. Gran would watch her and go into *tsk*ing overdrive.

Dad *had* to ditch the idea straightaway.

But even as my head was forming the thought, Dad was already on the phone to his client, telling the poor guy to reserve a table for seven, with a high chair too, please.

"Oh – unless you fancy coming with us?" he suddenly checked with Cormac.

Cormac pushed back his chair, ready to head downstairs and get set for a hard day's work doing, er, *dead*-people stuff, and shook his head sadly.

"Can't – it's my mum's birthday!" he mouthed at Dad, as he brushed toast crumbs off his suit and picked a bit of egg off his lapel. "Bye, Sadie! Bye and thanks for breakfast, Joan!"

"That's all right, Cormac!" Gran said brightly, appearing so instantly in the kitchen doorway that

I knew she had been very much earwigging. "Have a good day at, uh . . . the, um, office."

I guess she couldn't quite bring herself to say "Have a good day at the undertaker's", what with all the tragically bereaved relatives and *deadness* and everything.

But you know, at *that* precise moment, I convinced myself that I'd rather spend a week doing work experience with Cormac than go to the restaurant for a tea torture with my entire extended family.

Still . . . you know what they say: often when you dread something, it turns out to be not so bad.

Huh!

Well, whoever "they" are, by 8.45 p.m. that Saturday night, I wanted to sue them. It was every *bit* as bad as I dreaded it would be, with added drama.

Mainly because the Granny Wars commenced.

Be afraid; be *very* afraid. . .

"Ooh, this is nice!" Gran said, when we first settled down at our table in the restaurant, which was done up in muted shades of sand, beige and, er, sandy beige. Gran liked those sort of shades. She blended in with the décor very well. Not including the giant, oversized white paper lanterns, of course. The size of those just reminded me of Sonny's head. He'd already bored us rigid (OK, maybe that was just me) about his recording stint on Monday for the entire stroll to the restaurant.

"Hmmm . . . if you like that sort of thing, I suppose," Nonna vaguely responded to Gran's comment, tossing her purple-and-orange-patterned pashmina over her shoulder dismissively. "Of course, it hasn't got any of that wonderful Mediterranean atmosphere you get in the restaurants *I* go to in *Mo-ha-car*."

Gran pursed her neatly lipsticked lips. And we hadn't even seen the menu yet. Things were *only* just warming up.

By the time we had our starters, Gran seemed on the ropes. She was visibly shrinking with dislike as Nonna droned on and on about her many "dear, dear friends" in Spain.

And then Gran came back fighting.

"It's a wonderful thing to have friends, *Muriel*," Gran suddenly interrupted, feeding titbits of her melon starter to Martha, who'd whined the minute she saw the high chair and only quieted when she was plonked on Gran's knee. "But surely if you have such good friends, I'd have thought *one* of them would have offered to have you stay with them while the builders were in your flat?"

Nonna's nose flared, unaccustomed as she was to anyone tripping her up during one of her monologues, *or* calling her "Muriel".

Ding! Ding! went Dad's spoon on the side of his glass of beer, sounding like the bell in a boxing match. Was that deliberate? I shot a look at him but couldn't tell; his other hand was up, trying to catch the attention of a passing waitress, to ask how long the main course was going to take. A few seconds, I bet he was hoping, since the early attempts at granny-bonding weren't going too well.

Deliberate *ding! ding!* or not, with that dig about Nonna's friends, it was a case of Round One to *Gran*.

Nonna looked as if she was about to reply, but Sonny appeared back from a visit to the loo at that point and – completely oblivious to the tense atmosphere – launched into an impromptu impersonation of Frank Sinatra, whose voice was crooning some old, smooth, jazzy 1950s ballad from the hidden speakers in the background. As the track faded out, Sonny put an imaginary trilby on his head at a rakish angle, causing *both* my proud grandmothers to burst into spontaneous applause. Same went for a bunch of people at nearby tables who'd witnessed it too. Sonny did a few quick bows their way (*boy*, did he love an audience).

I spotted Mum smile with pleasure and relief, thrilled that Sonny had unwittingly got Gran and Nonna on the same team again.

Yeah, did she reckon? I silently put a bet on with myself about how long it would last. I guessed five minutes.

Wrong; it was thirty seconds.

Round Two began as Sonny sat down in his place next to Nonna.

"That was wonderful, Sonny! We should enter you on one of those *Stars In Their Eyes*-type programmes as a young Frank Sinatra!" said Gran, leaning over the table, eyes wide with wonder.

"Don't know about that, Gran," Sonny laughed, as Nonna snaked an arm territorially around his shoulders. "But it could be fun if the band did a cover of one of his songs in the future, though!"

Sonny acted like Sadie Rocks (urgh!) were headed for a long and fruitful career. *In your dreams, Sonny!* I said, but only in the privacy of my head. Flicking through Dad's monthly music magazines, I always found features about what people in bands were doing now. And it was more usually working for the Halifax Building Society than buying-my-fifth-luxury-yacht-and-headlining-Live-Aid-2028.

"Oh, now you've reminded me, Sonny! I have a Frank Sinatra compilation CD that I got out of Woolworth's a while ago!" Gran said excitedly, jiggling Martha on her knee. "I could lend it to you, if you want!"

Nonna dived in before Sonny could reply. "Actually, back at home in *Mo-ha-car* I have the most *wonderful* original box set of Frank Sinatra albums – they were my darling Jack's. Years ago, he said they were worth quite a lot of money, so they'd be worth *much* more now, of course. *You* can have them if you'd like, Sonny!"

"Wow! *Thanks!*" grinned Sonny, unaware of Gran deflating on the other side of the table.

The winner of *that* round: Nonna.

Round Three came as the main course was served: "Oh, I didn't know this came with calamari!" said Nonna, gazing down at the crispy, deep-fried rings on the side of her salmon. "That's *squid*, you know. We eat a lot of delicacies like this in Spain."

"Think you'll find they're plain old onion rings, *Muriel*," said Gran, crunching into one herself. (Winner: Gran.)

Round Four happened as Dad tried to act the host and pour everyone some more fizzy water. "Yes, please, Max, dear," said Gran, nodding at her empty glass.

"No – *still* water for me, Max. You'll find for the older person, fizzy water tends to give you . . . well . . . *gas*," said Know-It-All Nonna, pointedly letting her eyes drop to Gran's midriff, and winning herself a point.

By Round Five – pudding – I'd kind of lost the will to live, along with Dad, Mum, Will and Martha, whose whingeing had turned to outright whines and yells. I knew how she felt. The crotchety atmosphere had even managed to seep into Sonny's consciousness, and he was alternately talking (and endlessly talking) about his band's plans and frowning at the OAP sniping going on. Good grief; if they'd been thinking clearly, both our grannies would've been horrified to think that they were the cause of premature lines appearing on their precious grandson's forehead. . .

"Shush, shush, sweetie-pie!" Gran crooned as she tried to eat her tiramisu while gently rocking the buggy in an attempt to get Martha to realize that sleeping was a more pleasant option than screaming.

"Joan, the *best* thing is just to turn Martha away from you and ignore her," Nonna announced loudly. "She'll *never* go off to sleep if she has *you* paying her so much attention!"

"I *knew* we should've got a babysitter for her

instead of dragging her along here. . ." I heard Mum mutter to Will.

She was so right. It would have been a *much* more fun and relaxed evening if Nonna had been left at home with a babysitter.

"Nonsense!" said Nonna, hearing Mum's remark too. "In Spain, *all* the children come out in the evening with their parents for meals. They just have fun, then fall asleep in laps and in prams."

Yes, but perhaps they weren't traumatized by the bad vibes given off by duelling grandmothers.

"Fresh air normally gets her to sleep," I announced, standing up and offering my hands out to grab Martha. "I'll take her outside on the pavement for a bit."

"It'll be chilly! She'll need her hat and her little jacket!" said Gran, rummaging around in the buggy.

"Take this for her instead, Sadie, sweetheart," Nonna burst in competitively, sweeping the pashmina off her shoulders.

"We're fine," I said, resisting both offers in case I slighted someone. Instead, I slid the cardie off the back of my chair and draped it around both me and my fractious but adorable baby sister.

"Hey, if we hurry, we can be in Mexico by morning!" I whispered dumbly in Martha's tiny pink shell of an ear, as we wended our way through the packed, hectic restaurant and the muddle of customers who'd suddenly got up to shuffle around to the retro sounds.

Ah, the door.

Great: chilled air out here on the street.

Bliss . . . silence, except for the peaceful blast of passing traffic.

"What are they *like*?" I said softly to Martha, her big eyes blinking in wonder at the mixture of coolness and the star-like street lamps.

I gazed back inside, and could make out our table behind the throng of impromptu, smiling dancers. By comparison, from here my family all looked like they were attending a funeral. Maybe I could make a fortune hiring them out as rent-a-mourners to McConnell & Sons, if they ever had unpopular (dead) clients.

Urgh, this was zero fun.

With one hand, I wriggled my mobile out of my back pocket, thinking that I could phone and moan about the Granny Wars to either Hannah or Letty. I was momentarily quite proud of my mates; they might not like each other, and might try subtly to prove they were the best at being my best friend, but they'd never sunk so low as to snipe at each other, like my juvenile grannies were doing right now. . .

But whatever. Hannah and Letty's mobiles both flipped to answer-message, and I wasn't in the mood to ramble into nothingness.

I had to do *something* more positive.

Faintly, I could make out the track that had started blasting away inside: it was that funky Mark Ronson track, where a Coldplay song's covered in a big-band style.

I punched in a number on my mobile.

"Don't talk – just listen," I ordered, as soon as a voice said hello.

I spotted Sonny turning round in his seat, his mobile pressed to his ear.

"No! Don't look at me either!" I barked.

Sonny spun round.

I could see Gran and Nonna both suddenly gazing at him, small, curious smiles on their faces as they beheld the Golden Child.

And what do you know: only *he* could help end this tense evening on a happy note.

Well, thanks to *me*, but no one *else* had to know that.

I told Sonny what he needed to do.

"*Twirl* them," I said ominously.

"What?" he squeaked.

I spelt it out more clearly, in an idiot-friendly way, knowing that Gran and Nonna would *love* it.

"*Twirl* them! Rock 'n' roll style! At the same time!!"

He got it. He wasn't an all-dancing, all-singing, all-performing stage-school brat for nothing.

Ten seconds later, Sonny had cajoled both our grans to their feet and had grabbed them each by a hand, spinning them out and then back under his arms to the irresistible remix track.

Nonna and Gran couldn't help breathlessly giggling, I could see that. And Mum, Will and Dad were laughing along too (phew) as they watched Sonny spin the formerly truculent old "girls".

"Look – I did it!" I laughed to Martha.

But she was zonked – fast asleep and snoring like a kitten.

"Yay for me," I said softly, since no one else seemed to be aware of (or was bothered to argue over) *my* existence tonight. . .

Real names and real shame

There's a girl in my class called Suzanne Hannett (mega-sporty, and very freckly in a cute, pretty way).

So this one time, Suzanne's dad and his girlfriend tried to get permission to take her out of school during term time, and our head teacher made them feel like criminals.

It was like they'd written a letter asking to take Suzanne on a road trip round America with the aim of robbing gas stations and indiscriminately shooting innocent bystanders.

What they *actually* wanted to do was get married in the Maldives.

They got hauled in for a serious chat with the head about the importance of Suzanne's education; yeah, like five extra days off would mean she'd *never* stand a chance of getting to university and she'd *never* be an astrophysicist or a neuro-surgeon or whatever thanks to their careless parenting.

(She wants to be a trapeze artist in Cirque du Soleil, by the way.)

Anyway, that's what it's like at our school, and every other regular school, I guess (Hannah says parents at *her* school practically needed *counselling* after being grilled by their head over term-time absences).

It's not like that at Sonny's *stage* school.

Kennedy Watson is Sonny's best mate (real name Kenneth; big dumb plate-sized face; big head to match). When he got an audition last week to be in an ad for bathroom air fresheners which hide dubious whiffs, the stage-school head was apparently practically *pushing* him out of the door, wishing him luck and telling him not to hurry back.

Which is why Sonny's band had no problem getting a whole day off to record their first single today. And I guess it helped too that their manager, Benny, was a lecturer from the same school.

Through a big glass window, I could see Benny in the other room now, chatting earnestly to Sonny, Kennedy and the other three members of the band. I couldn't hear what he was saying, though – the sound on the mixing desk had been turned down by the producer or whoever he was who had just gone out for a break. Poor guy . . .

after a day of listening to the same rotten song over and over again, he probably needed to go away and lie down in a quiet room to recover.

Still, there was one more take to go, apparently – and I'd got here after school just in time to catch it.

Don't know why I was bothering really, since I didn't like. . .

a) boy bands
b) any of the band's tracks I'd heard so far, or
c) Sonny's dumb friend Kennedy, who I could see picking his nose right now (wow – future fans would go *mad* for that).

So why *was* I here? Well, I guess. . .

a) I was curious – I'd passed this recording studio in Highbury like a gazillion times, and Dad had told me that a whole bunch of famous bands had recorded here over the years
b) Sonny had asked me to come, really nicely and everything. Which was surprising, and kind of cool, and probably down to the fact that he knew my spin-the-grannies trick on Saturday night had been a work of genius, and

c) it might be funny to watch, in an excruciating way.

"Hey, if they go for a break," said Cormac, nodding at the band, "we could sneak in there and do a duet – *you* could be the new Beyonce and *I* could be the new Jay-Z!"

I shot a cynical sideways glance at Cormac. I knew for sure that I look about as much like Beyonce as my cat, Dog, looks like an exotic snow leopard. But in his fresh-from-a-burial funeral suit (groooo. . .), Cormac looked about as much like a successful multi-millionaire rapper as Clyde, my rabbit.

"I don't *think* so," I muttered, raising one eyebrow at him in a sarcastic arch. (It was the right eyebrow. Whenever I try to raise my *left* eyebrow, the muscle goes into spasm and it looks like a hairy brown caterpillar on my forehead is trembling madly. Which doesn't exactly convey a lot of attitude.)

"Come on!" Cormac jokingly encouraged me, nudging a rangy elbow into my side. "That producer guy will hear us and get all excited at discovering us, and next thing we'll have a hit single that outsells Sadie Rocks! Fancy it?"

"Nah," I said, with a shake of my head and a

shiver down my spine (that happened every time I heard the name of Sonny's band). "But I quite fancy running over there and twiddling all the knobs while no one's looking, though!"

Me and Cormac both glanced at the huge mixing deck and its mysteriously complicated series of buttons and sliding doodahs.

"Feels like we're on the flight deck of a spaceship!" said Cormac, shuffling himself into a more comfy position on the super-slidey 1970s-style vinyl sofa.

"Maybe there's a knob on there that vaporizes people when they hit a bad note," I suggested.

Cormac laughed, which was kind of brilliant, considering he watched wall-to-wall comedy DVDs when he wasn't busy burying people.

Hurray for him laughing, and hurray for Sonny inviting him along today too – or I might not be sitting here.

It's just that I know I come across as the queen of sarcasm a lot of the time, but really, there's a small, fearsomely shy five-year-old person living somewhere inside my body. And this afternoon – as I walked towards the recording studio – that small, fearsomely shy person had been shouting, "*Noooo!* You're only thirteen and can't go wandering into a recording studio on your own! Run away!!*"

Without the company of Letty or Hannah, or the distraction of Letty and Hannah together, slightly ignoring each other, I probably (definitely) *would've* trudged off as fast as my Converse trainers would take me. Which is not that fast, as I wear them turned down at the heel, like slip-ons.

But then – *phew* – I spotted Cormac coming bounding along the pavement towards me, like some weird cartoon character in his skinny black suit and matching tie, white shirt and red, red hair.

Cormac might be blushingly shy in social circumstances sometimes, but he's the opposite of me and has this confident forty-year-old person inside him, who handles death and stressed-out relatives with ease. So walking up and buzzing the intercom of the recording studio was a no-brainer.

And in I slunk behind him, very, very glad indeed to have Cormac McConnell as a friend. . .

"What are the names of the other lads again?" asked Cormac. "Their *real* names, I mean."

"Well, you know already that Kennedy's Kenneth, right? And that guy is Marcus, but his real name's Mark," I explained, pointing at the boys, from left to right. "*He's* Hal, but his real name's Alan, and Ziggy is the one at the end, but he's really Gordon."

"It's nuts, isn't it? That the stage school people can just decide what is and isn't a cool name," Cormac muttered thoughtfully.

"Could've been worse," I shrugged. "My nonna could have had a go at renaming them. They could've ended up as Thor, Kensington, *Mo-ha-car*, Heathcliff and Zebedee."

"Right – I'm going to use that somehow!" Cormac announced, taking a small black notebook and pen out of his inside jacket pocket. He'd already scribbled down some of the Granny War stuff that had happened on Saturday night, for future use in a comedy routine.

"Are you going to do another gig in the park soon, then?" I asked, since it seemed relevant.

Cormac's impromptu comedy routines on Sunday mornings in Highbury Fields park; the couple he'd done so far had been fun, and I (and the small, fearsomely shy person who lived inside me) really admired his nerve for standing up and doing it.

"Yeah. . ." said Cormac, nodding slowly as he wrote in his notebook. "Might do it *this* Sunday. Might ask a few of my old mates along too. . ."

Oooh, I hadn't met any of Cormac's friends

yet. He'd hinted that he'd sort of lost touch with them a bit since he'd left school and gone into the family firm. Seemed some of them thought his family's firm was pretty odd, but thought it was even odder that he'd want to actually *work* for it.

"Right!" said the producer bloke, suddenly bounding into the room with a clap of his hands. He slid up a button doodah on the desk and cheerfully barked: "Ready for a last take, then, guys?"

The five boys sprang away from Benny and got back to their places by their various mikes. Benny left them and came to join us in the room with the mixing desk and the squeaky vinyl sofa.

Sitting on the vinyl sofa, it was as if me and Cormac were invisible; neither the producer or Benny took any notice of us, as they concentrated on the performance the band were just about to give.

But *someone* noticed us: Sonny. He was biting his lip, lost in concentration, when he stared straight ahead and spotted us lurking in the background of the other room.

He gave us a hurried smile and a wave and then went back to biting his lip, looking down at the floor, deep in thought. Wow – was he ill? Had someone turned down his enthusiasm button or something? He didn't look his usual, mega-enthusiastic self. Nerves, I guess. The last take; the last chance to get it right.

All of a sudden, I felt a tiny ping in my chest, and for a second, couldn't figure out what it was.

Indigestion, maybe? The casserole at school today was pretty disgusting. . .

But nope: what it was dawned on me as I checked out Sonny, standing slightly agitatedly by his mike, gathering himself together.

The ping was a mixture of excitement and – can't believe I'm going to admit this – a little bit of *pride* in my baby brother. (I'm older than him by seven minutes. Important fact.)

I think the ping had happened for several reasons: for a start, the band weren't wearing their stupid neon cycling-short outfits or doing their dumb dance routine – they were just dressed in normal jeans and T-shirt-type stuff, and were standing mostly still, if you didn't count an edgy twitch or two.

Also, with Sonny ditching the bouncy, annoying hyper-confidence for once and coming across a little nervous, it made me sort of want to . . . well . . . *hug* him (can't believe I said that either).

Yep, all of a sudden, I really did feel for him – the way I once did when he split his chin falling off a seesaw (aged three) and had to go to hospital and get stitches.

"Come on . . . do a good job!" I mouthed silently, as I heard the intro music start up.

All the endless rehearsing had obviously paid off. The boys launched into perfect harmony on a ballad I'd never heard before.

The singing was great.

But the song . . . it was the most awful, slushy *dirge* I'd ever heard in my life.

"*Love, it's a lovely word, but it's not easy for a boy like me to sayyyyyyy. . .*" (Kennedy sang that bit, with the others crooning "*Love is lovely, love is lovely*" in the background.)

Beside me, I could feel Cormac's shoulders shuddering up and down as he struggled not to laugh.

If the first verse made me grind my teeth down to stumps with embarrassment, things only got worse (much worse) with the chorus.

"*Oooooh, Momma, you always looked after me, and Dad, you're the man I wanna grow up to be, 'cause we are – yeah! Familyyyy!!*" all five boys sang together.

"*Hey, love ya, Mom and Dad!*" Kennedy rapped at the end.

Instead of wanting to (yuck) *hug* Sonny, I

suddenly knew I'd have to change my name by deed poll to escape the shame. I'd also have to have facial plastic surgery, ask the police if they could grant me a new identity and move me to a safe house, and deny I'd ever been related to the boy singing second from the right.

How could I ever live this down?

Pity this *wasn't* the flight deck of an alien spacecraft. Or I could've leant over and found the knob marked "Vaporize!" and got rid of the band and the song with one swift *tweak*. . .

Down with weasels

I looked at the Weasel.

The Weasel looked at me.

I quickly walked past the living-room doorway and followed Hannah towards the kitchen at the back of the house.

"I thought you said he was going to some after-school club or something?" I hissed urgently at her.

I like Hannah a lot. I like hanging out with Hannah. I just didn't like hanging out at Hannah's house when her weaselly ten-year-old brother, Harry, was around. In fact, I'd told her on numerous occasions that I never wanted to be within a twenty-kilometre radius of him as long as I lived. She understood. She felt the same way, but of course, being closely related to him, she couldn't do much about it.

Me and Hannah once had a conversation about how tragic it was that press-ganging had been outlawed a hundred or so years ago. I mean *yes*, kidnapping young men and boys to work on sailing ships that went on voyages that often took years *was* terribly cruel and unjust, but then the long-ago politicians who banned it had never met *Harry*. . .

"It was an after-school karate club. He got banned," Hannah sighed, opening the fridge up and rummaging inside. "I didn't know till today. Actually, Mum didn't know till today either – Harry hid the letter saying he was banned."

"What did he get banned for?" I asked, nervously glancing back towards the living room, then quickly gazing around the kitchen for any booby traps.

"Well, you know how people wear those white pyjama-ish suits for karate, and then have all those coloured belts, depending what level they're at?" said Hannah, taking out a carton of cranberry juice.

"Uh-huh," I said, carefully sitting down on a high stool by the breakfast bar (checking first that the stool didn't have one leg shorter than the other or margarine smeared on the top of it).

"Well, Harry took all the belts and hid them for a laugh."

Have you heard of Tourette's syndrome? Where someone can't stop themselves from swearing?

Well, I sometimes wondered if Harry had a form of Tourette's that made him unable to resist doing obnoxious practical jokes and indulging in general horrible behaviour.

Still, after such gems as putting cling film over the toilet seat (that caught *me* out) and trying to take a photo of a dead person (he snuck past Cormac at McConnell & Sons for that one), hiding a few karate belts didn't sound *too* bad.

"He hid them in a cistern in the boys' toilets," said Hannah, with a roll of her eyes. She tucked a long, stray, straight lock of hair behind her ear as she poured us both a drink.

"Nice!" I muttered, imagining the soggy tangle of cotton belts, the colours probably bleeding together.

"So . . . what's new?" asked Hannah, as she pulled out a stool from the other side of the breakfast bar – and then stopped, picked off the prickly holly leaf that had been Blu-tacked on there and sat herself down. She made no comment about it. Harry's practical jokes were so much part of her daily routine that only the truly terrible ones were worth acknowledging.

From a drawer to the right of the breakfast bar, she pulled out a couple of stripy straws for us both.

"Well, there's good news and bad news," I told her, taking one of the straws and sucking up a big glug of cranberry.

"Bad news first, then," Hannah said, grinning at me. I'd sent her an email on Sunday, telling her about the Saturday-night Granny Wars, and she'd written back immediately, demanding more news of my nutty nans. It was Tuesday now and she probably thought that I was about to tell her the next instalment. I wasn't; Gran had stayed well away from our house so far this week (which must have been tough, since she was so besotted with little Martha).

"OK," I said, getting ready to splurge. "This morning, I caught Mum screaming into a pillow in her room, after I heard Nonna telling Mum that she really, really admired her for not caring that she's a dress size bigger than she used to be." When Mum clocked me watching her, she pretended she was just sniffing the pillow, and claimed she'd then just sneezed into it a *yelling* sort of way.

But *I'd* heard. *I* knew.

Wish Mum didn't feel she had to hide stuff from me. . .

"Aw, but that's a bit mean of your, er, nonna!!" muttered Hannah, stumbling on the name. "Fancy a biscuit?"

"Yes, please," I answered, as I watched my friend slip off the stool to go rummage in a cupboard for the cookie jar. "Also, we *still* have to watch the titchy TV and get eye strain, 'cause Will ordered a new cable for the big telly, but it won't be here till the end of the week."

"What a *pain*," murmured Hannah, shuffling a few mugs and a sugar bowl aside to get at the jar. "You can always come and watch telly *here* anytime you want to, though!"

Letty had made me the same offer, and I'd definitely take her up on it. A fact that I didn't mention to Hannah, in case she got huffy about me turning down *her* offer. But then Letty didn't have a weasel for a brother.

"Thanks, *but*. . ." I nodded my head in the direction of the living room and the weasel currently lurking ominously in there.

"Oh, *right*. Of course. I understand," said Hannah, getting my point. "So any other bad news?

"What, apart from the fact that my old room *still* hasn't dried out after the water tank burst, even though Will's stuck a heater in there twenty-four hours a day?"

I felt like using up a chunk of my allowance and buying another heater from wherever you buy heaters from, just to speed up the process.

Oh, to have my own empty, silent, shoeless, snoreless, un-cave-like room to doss down in for the next ten days or whatever.

"And did I tell you that my cat is going crazy, stuck in her cage for so long, and has started to do that scary repetitive walking-back-and-forth thing that animals in zoos do?"

Nearly two months: that's how long ago Sonny had kicked Dog off the garden wall with a poorly aimed football. The big nerk.

"Wow! Poor Dog!" frowned Hannah, coming back to the breakfast bar with the cookie jar. "How much longer has she got to stay in there?"

"She's been in for seven weeks, so one more – if she doesn't stage a prison break in the meantime," I told her. "We've got to take her to the vet next Saturday to get her leg checked over, and if the torn ligaments have mended, hopefully she'll be free."

Free to claw Nonna's suitcases and curl up and shed hair on her pashminas, I bet. Uh-oh.

"Anything else? Bad, I mean?" asked Hannah, settling herself down on the stool again.

There was. I'd already told it to Letty at break yesterday morning, but again – no point mentioning that to Hannah, in case she thought she was getting second-hand news.

"Well, just the fact that my brother's band are

releasing the most nauseating song in the known universe, and it makes me feel like *barfing*."

Benny asked me and Cormac to leave before the band came out of the recording room yesterday. He said he needed to have a "debrief" with them on their own. I think it was more that *he* knew that *we* knew the song was sheer pants, and didn't want the lads to come out and see our shocked and stunned faces. Or maybe he didn't trust us not to burst out laughing if Sonny or any of the others asked us what we thought of it.

I think Sonny knew too – he didn't ask me *anything* when he finally got home.

I did mutter something about him being good at harmonies (true) when Nonna pestered us both for details. And I was pretty interested to hear him tell Nonna that there'd been a last-minute change of plan about what should be the single.

Well, *that* made sense. Sonny had a pretty big head, but there was surely no *way* he'd have willingly invited an audience to watch the band recording *that* sugary-sweet drivel. . .

"Yeah, you said it was rotten when you phoned yesterday. What a shame!" said Hannah, pushing the cookie jar into the middle of the breakfast bar between us. She held her hand out, indicating that I could have first pick, since my need for the medicinal cure of sugary biscuits was greater than hers. "And what's the good news?"

"My fringe sat OK today," I shrugged.

At the same time, I tugged at the cookie jar lid, wondering what delights would be inside. Hannah's mum might've had a few value packs of beans and toilet roll in the house, but she generally – yay! – didn't scrimp when it came to biscuits.

Pwooooffff!

The sound was soft; softer than a clump of fresh snow falling off a branch into a snowdrift; softer than a marshmallow dropping from Martha's fat little fingers on to the floor.

It was the *pwooooffff!* of a billowing cloud of chalky whiteness, puffing out of the cookie jar and settling on the breakfast bar surface, and all over our faces and hair.

How the Weasel had wedged the thin cling-film parcel of flour between the jar and its lid, I wasn't entirely sure.

And how he'd fixed it so that that yanking the lid open would *tear* the thin cling-film parcel of flour and cause a near-silent mini-explosion was anyone's guess.

I blinked at Hannah, my eyelashes heavy with Homepride's finest self-raising flour. Her face might have been as pale as a white-faced clown, but I could tell from her eyes that underneath, her cheeks were blazing red.

"*HARRRRYYYY!!!*" she yelled, jumping off her stool and stomping off through the house.

I'd been meaning to chat to Hannah about Cormac: about his next planned stand-up spot this coming weekend, and the fact that his maybe-not-so-great mates might be coming along.

But I'd save that for another day. I needed every bit of my energy to cope with the confusing crush of Nonnas at home, and so right now, I wanted to be as far away from the Weasel and his tiring "jokes" as possible.

Calmly, I stretched over and tore off a piece of kitchen roll to clean my face with. Then just as calmly, I picked up what was left of my cranberry juice and poured it into one of the boy-sized trainers that had been kicked off and left by the kitchen radiator.

"Catch up with you later, Hannah!" I called out, glancing into the living room as I let myself out.

I was pleased to see that my friend had the situation well under control. Harry was so squashed under the oversized cushion Hannah was pressing down on him that he looked as if he was being eaten alive by the sofa.

Oh, if *only* dreams came true. . .

Things that go flump in the night

There are impossible dreams.

Dreams about carnivorous sofas scoffing horrible boys.

Dreams about nonnas who get laryngitis and sit quietly in your living room, looking lovely, smiling serenely at everyone and wordlessly hugging *all* their grandchildren in rotation.

There are dreams about brothers who stop embarrassing you by tap-dancing in the middle of Woolworth's and singing in corny junior boy bands, and instead turn to religion and train as monks.

There are dreams about becoming a world-famous comedy double act with tall, lanky trainee funeral directors, touring the globe and having comedy legends like Harry Hill and Billy Connelly get down on their knees and do "We are not worthy!" bows and scrapes to you.

Sigh. . .

Like I say, impossible dreams.

Then there are dreams that seem almost *real*.

Like the one last night, where I dreamt I was having the most delicious, sinking-into-a-cloud, peaceful sleep, though in the miraculously-dried-out spare room. In my almost-real dream, the room was wonderfully empty, apart from me and my blow-up bed; the moonlight was streaming through the window (no bat-cave darkness); and it only smelled a *tiny* bit of damp.

And then I woke up.

I don't know what woke me first: Nonna's snoring, the fact that my hip had gone painfully numb thanks to my blow-up bed semi-deflating and basically leaving me sleeping on the hard floor, or the strange *FLUMP!* from somewhere along the corridor.

"Huh?!" I said, sitting up so sharply in bed that Clyde hopped off my thigh – where he'd been sleeping – and indignantly gave my left thumb a nip.

"Ouch!"

The "huh?!" and the "ouch!" weren't particularly loud, but they were enough to wake Nonna up. Amazing, really, when she could sleep through her own vibrating road drill of a snorefest *and* the sound of weird, unexplained flumping.

"What?! What's going on!" Nonna flustered, in the pitch-black gloom of my room.

"I heard a *FLUMP!*" I told her.

Nonna chuckled a bit.

"Don't!" I said, slightly irked. "It could be a *burglar!*"

"Sadie, darling – I think burglars go *CRASH!*, rather than *FLUMP!*"

"You don't know that for sure!" I said, suddenly feeling as indignant as Clyde did when I vaulted him off my leg just now. "They might go *FLUMP!* when they're . . . well . . . when they're. . ."

My mind flailed around for a viable reason for a burglar to go *FLUMP!*, but the only thing that popped into my head was the vision of someone dressed in one of those dumb, blow-up sumo wrestling suits, rifling through our drawers and bumping into the furniture.

Uh-oh – that started me off giggling too.

"What?" asked Nonna, with an obvious smile in her voice.

I couldn't answer for giggling. I was now picturing my sumo burglar stranded on his back like a beetle, arms and legs paddling uselessly in the air as he struggled to get up off the floor. . .

OK, so it probably wouldn't have made me laugh so much in the cold light of day, but there was something about being sleep-deprived for so long that was making me slightly *hysterical*, I think.

Whatever, it was infectious. Next thing, Nonna started chuckling some more too.

And so there we were, Nonna and me, sniggering like schoolgirls on a sleepover, as though there wasn't fifty years' difference between us, and as though she never in a million years drove me mad.

Pity she couldn't sack some of her other personalities and let this one hang around more. I liked *this* Nonna a lot.

"OK, listen, Sadie. . ." she said, as the sniggers start to ease off. "We haven't heard any more *flumping* noises in the last few minutes. Are you sure that you weren't just dreaming?"

"Well, *maybe*," I answered, shrugging at her in the gloom, reckoning that if I was hysterical enough to giggle so much over so little, I probably *was* tired enough to imagine things going *FLUMP!* in the night. "Got to nip to the loo. . ."

SQUELCH! *PPPPPPFFFFTTTT!!*

We both started sniggering some more, at the vaguely rude noises my semi-deflated bed made as I struggled to stand up and wobble off it. The struggling and the wobbling made me thump into a couple of painful corners of furniture as I tried to feel my way to the bedroom door. (Could've done with my own protective blow-up sumo burglar suit.)

I thought about asking Nonna to put the bedroom light on for me, and then stopped myself – she might spot Clyde flopping around.

Yesterday evening, I'd promised the lesser-known Neurotic Nonna – through gritted teeth – that I'd keep Clyde in his normally unused hutch in the garden at nights. (She was still wittering on about allergies and Lyme disease, even though she hadn't shown any allergic reactions to him or Dog at all. Another thing she hadn't done was read the document I'd downloaded about the true cause of Lyme disease.)

"Careful, sweetie!" Nonna laughed as I bumped. "If the others hear all the racket you're making, they really *will* think there's a burglar!"

I heard the snap of elastic as I finally slipped out the door – Nonna was pinging her eye mask back into place, as if the gloom in the room wasn't enough for her.

Out in the hall, just like in my dream, the moonlight flooded through a window. It seemed so bright after the bat cave that I didn't feel the need to flick switches on and blind myself with 100-watt lightbulbs.

After a quick wee in the cool of the bathroom, I suddenly found myself thinking about the dream again . . . the one about my old room being dry and habitable. There was no whirring to hear – Will had switched the fan heater off for the night – but how was the drying out coming along?

I padded along the carpeted hall, with my fingers crossed hopefully.

Ahead of me, I spotted a rabbit-shaped shadow bounding into my old room. Hey, maybe Clyde was psychic as well as grumpy. Maybe he'd sensed that I was going to check the carpet for dampness. Maybe he thought he'd get there first and help by hopping around to test for squelchiness underfoot.

There was no moonlight on this side of the house, and the blind at the window was three-quarters pulled down, letting in only the faintest orange glow from a street lamp.

But it was enough for me to know where I was without resorting to the overhead light. Slipping just inside the bedroom door, I crouched down and felt around blindly, pleased to sense, well, no wetness.

My heart gave a little leap. I might have had a small oasis of fun with Nonna just now, but that didn't make up for the wall-to-wall snoring. (She'd started up already – I could hear her from here.) What I meant was, I could drag some of my stuff through to this room tomorrow morning and make it pretty cosy and comf—

FLUMPPPP!!

Quick as if I'd been electrocuted, I straightened up and flipped the light switch. That *FLUMPPPP!* sounded dangerously close to hand.

"Squeak!!"

The sudden flood of light showed a startled rabbit, perched on a soggy pile of plaster on the carpet (the cause of the first *FLUMP!*). Great – the leak from the tank in the loft had been fixed pretty quick, but all the escaping water must've soaked into the ceiling, like a soggy sponge cake that finally collapsed.

A *second* soggy pile of plaster had *FLUMPPPP!!*ed on to the floor near the window, with a damp puff of sticky white dust swirling up from it.

I glanced up at the bare, gaping wooden slats in the ceiling, where the plaster was meant to be, then reached down and scooped up Clyde, gently brushing the clinging dust off his head and whiskers. (I'd wished someone could've done that to me yesterday. I hadn't managed to get all the flour off my face before I left Hannah's, and got some very bizarre glances on the way home.)

My first reaction was (of course) to go and shake Mum and Will awake. But then I looked at the ceiling again and realized there was no more of it to come down, and all that would happen was that they'd get out of bed, gasp, be able to do nothing till morning, when they could put in a call to a local, friendly plasterer, and then go *back* to bed, all frazzled and wide awake.

Maybe it was kindness that made me decide not to disturb them.

Or maybe it was more that *I* was now wide awake and quite fancied having the whole of the middle-of-the-night house to myself for a little while.

"Come on – I'll treat you to a carrot," I whispered in Clyde's large, floppy ear, as I flipped off the light and headed downstairs. "I hear they're very good for shock."

I wasn't exactly in shock, like Clyde, but I decided to treat myself to something anyway; maybe to help me get over the disappointment of not moving into the spare room tomorrow.

And so five minutes later, I was lying on a pile of cushions next to Dog's cage, feeding her slices of ham from a packet I'd found in the fridge while I helped myself from the big bag of nachos I'd rifled from the cupboard.

"Weird, isn't it?" I said to my imprisoned cat. "Sonny could *be* on that, one day soon!"

I was nodding at the doll-sized TV in the corner of the room. Of course, what I meant was that Sonny – and Kennedy and co. – could be on telly in *general*, not that *particular* one. (If I had to watch my brother mime his awful song on some programme, I'd rather watch it on a TV that was big enough not to need binoculars to watch.)

I was sure Dog understood; she just chose to show that she agreed with me by trying to eat my fingers as well as the latest slice of ham.

Clyde hopped closer to join in on the conversation.

"I mean, I *would* be *sort* of proud of him," I whispered to my trusty pets, "*if* his band was any good. And *if* he didn't show off about it so much. And *if* my grans and mum and dad and Will and everyone would stop acting like he's some kind of *genius* all of the time. . ."

The way Clyde nudged my knee aside with his nose to get to the last chunk of carrot, I knew he sympathized. Sort of.

Dog suddenly didn't seem quite so sure about that last point, though; she was crinkling up her nose and shaking her head.

"Oh, sorry!" I muttered, suddenly realizing I'd

offered her a chilli nacho instead of a piece of ham.

I was getting in a muddle.

I was probably more tired than I realized.

Maybe I should go back to my squelching, *pfffffft*-ing bed. . .

"Sadie?"

I opened my eyes, and panicked for a second, thinking that the eyesight in my left eye had gone – till my sleepy senses kicked in and I realized I had a floppy rabbit ear spread over that side of my face, like a furry eyepatch.

Out of my right eye, I could see Nonna, in a bright orange and rusty red kaftan, a cup of tea clutched in her hands, and the bright blast of morning light framing her pink foam rollers like a marshmallow halo.

"Oh, hi, Nonna!" I mumbled, sitting up and feeling the sensation of nacho crumbs falling off my chest. I must have startled a deeply snoozing Clyde too – he gave me a grumpy nip on the finger. Again.

"Oww!"

"Right – I'm having a word with your mum about this, Sadie," Nonna *tsk*ed. "In Spain, animals live outside, and with good reason."

She swept her arm out, as if to indicate the

mess of me, carrot and nacho crumbs, or maybe it was the fact that Clyde had bitten me (slightly) and Dog had her paw through the bars of her cage, frantically trying to get a claw into the empty packet of ham that she'd just spotted.

It didn't look great.

"A young girl like you can't be up half the night, playing with these animals and falling asleep on the floor, when you have a day's school in front of you!" Nonna nagged some more. "And you can't have a little baby like Martha coming into an environment like this, full of germs!"

So.

No Funny Nonna this morning, then.

Or maybe I just dreamt her too. . .?

The shiny-toy trick

"*One, two, three, twelve, five; once I caught a slug alive!*" I sang, as I juggled a cooing Martha on my lap. "*Six, seven, four, one, ten; then I let it ooze again!*"

Here's the thing: I'm shallow – I admit it. I get bored really easily and need to find dumb ways to entertain myself.

I mean, I love my baby sister with all my heart and a little bit more, but *boy* do I get brain-drainingly *bored* singing the same old nursery rhymes to her over and over again.

Which is why I change the words around, just to entertain myself. And what did *she* know? At eight months old, you could sing the phone book to Martha and she'd probably love it, as long as you put it to a cute tune.

So far this Wednesday afternoon, I'd entertained her with "Baa, Baa, Black Bin", "This Little Piggy Went To Tesco", "Hickory Dickory Boing" and

"Incy-Wincey Meerkat" and she'd clapped her chubby little hands together for more.

"Sadie, you're just going to *confuse* little Martha," Gran said, tutting at me, a pile of newly ironed clothes in her arms. (I think she thought Rule No. 34 in *The Grandmas' Rule Book* was "*When on a visit to your family, you must never ignore a household chore that needs doing.*")

Gran is really lovely, but she's pretty straight. Put it this way: if she was asked to list her hobbies, they'd be cleaning, watching reruns of *The Weakest Link*, and reading the Lakeland homewares catalogue ("Ooh, *that* set of plastic food tubs is *very* good value!!").

Anytime I tried dropping one of my sarky remarks in her hearing, she tended to take them completely literally. ("Oh, *I* didn't know you loved cabbage, Sadie! Would you like some more?!")

As for any attempts at surreal humour . . . they just sailed *right* over the top of her head and kept going.

"Come on, now, Joan!" said Nonna, glancing up from the magazine she'd been flicking through. (In *her* version of *The Grandmas' Rule Book*, No. 34 read, "*When on a visit to your family, you must relax as much as possible and never refuse any cups of tea going.*") "Sadie's just using her imagination and being creative, aren't you, darling?"

I'd have appreciated Nonna's support, if it didn't mean she was using it as another point-scoring tool against Gran.

"Mmm," I mumbled non-committally, as Martha grabbed a fistful of my cheek and squeezed painfully.

After the Saturday Granny Wars, I'd thought Gran would stay well away from our place for the duration of Nonna's visit, but I guess she missed us – or maybe the chores she kept herself busy with – too much to stay away. Still, if Nonna had her way, Gran might throw down the laundry (OK, leave it in a neat pile) and head off in a huff soon enough. *Sigh*. . .

"Ah, and here's my *other* creative grandchild!" Nonna crooned, opening her arms to Sonny as he stode into the kitchen, fresh from another exhausting day doing the splits or miming being a street lamp, or whatever else they did in classes at stage school. "Give your nonna a hug, my darling! Ahh, that's lovely. Now, since you're standing, d'you fancy pouring me another cup of tea?"

Gran made the tiniest of sniffing noises – so tiny you could almost have missed it. But she might as well have yelled, "Get up and get it yourself, you lazy woman, and it wouldn't kill you to lend a hand and do a little something round the house to help out!"

And with that, Gran stomped away, her teetering pile of ironing clamped in her capable arms.

"Nobody else home?" asked Sonny, glancing around as he lifted the teapot and poured lukewarm Earl Grey into Nonna's mug.

"Mum's got a meeting at school, and Will's taking the ceiling to the tip," I told him, peeling five determined fingers from my face.

Will's mission was genuine (he was relocating five garden sackfuls of soggy plaster from the spare-room floor), but I wasn't entirely sure that Mum's was. I kind of suspected she'd made up the meeting, and was walking slowly and reluctantly home, trailing her handbag on the ground behind her, like a schoolkid who knows they're going to get into some serious trouble from their mum when they get home.

"Anyway, Sonny, darling," said Nonna, brushing away our dull exchange with one hand. "I've been terribly bored today. I went to the Tate Gallery and it was full of the most *awful* stuff that's supposed to be art!"

"Like I told you, you went to Tate *Modern*, instead of the Tate *Britain*," I said, shooting a grin at Sonny, who grinned right back. How funny; me and the Nerk were bonding over Know-It-All Nonna!

Anyway, the thing is, Tate Britain is this gallery full of amazing old-and-very-famous paintings. Tate Modern is full of amazing abstract art and deeply weird installations that I knew Nonna would *hate*.

"Well, of *course* it was easy to get muddled," said Nonna, taking a sip of her tea, "because they've *both* got the same name. What's the point in that? And when I used to visit London years ago, there was only *one* Tate gallery."

See? Everyone and everything was wrong except Nonna. Even a giant, world-famous gallery full of highly regarded modern artwork.

"Still, let's not talk about anything irritating," said Nonna, sounding faintly irritated. "Tell me instead about your day, Sonny. Any more news on your record, and when it's coming out? Can I buy it before I go back to Spain?"

"Uh, no," said Sonny, grabbing a packet of biscuits out of the cupboard and settling himself down at the table.

"*Bihhhh*. . ." gurgled Martha, leaning forward towards the rustly orange packet.

Weird; she'd never had a Jaffa Cake in her (so-far-short) life, and yet some treat-seeking gene was alerting her to the fact that what Sonny had was something she would definitely like. And I had a strong feeling that her first words weren't going to be "Mummy" or "Daddy" but "chocolate HobNob".

"The single won't be out for weeks," explained Sonny, doing a magic trick by making a Jaffa Cake disappear in one bite. He also made the packet disappear by holding it under the table, out of Martha's line of vision. "But the record company have had a sort of idea, Benny says."

"Which is?" asked Nonna, leaning an elbow on the table, drinking in his every word.

Ha – Martha might not know a genuine nursery rhyme from a boredom-busting made-up version, but she knew that Sonny was playing a trick on her. She practically launched herself backwards out of my lap in an attempt to look under the table to see where the packet of biscuits had gone.

"Well," I heard Sonny begin, as I wrestled my small but surprisingly heavy sister upright again (had Will been feeding her powdered *bricks* in her porridge?), "in the run-up to the single coming out, the record company thinks we should go and play some mini-gigs in schools around North London, just to get ourselves known, and get some fans, maybe."

"Oooh, what a fun idea!" said Nonna, clapping her hands together.

"Yeah, just as long as you don't come anywhere

near *my* school!" I warned Sonny, pointing a finger at him menacingly and then realizing it had a multi-coloured, frog-shaped teething ring dangling from it.

I don't know whether he was smiling at the teething ring or the fact that I was threatening him with it, but whatever – before he could give me a cheeky reply, he was distracted by the sound of Mum's key in the door.

"Ah, is there some tea on the go?" Mum asked, coming into the kitchen and spotting the teapot on the table. "I'd love a cup. . ."

I quickly glanced at her handbag, to check for signs of dragging. There were none that I could see. Maybe she'd had a meeting *after* all. She scooped up Martha from me, who in turn was delighted to see her mummy, and grabbed a happy handful of her cheek to prove it.

"Me too!" trilled Nonna. "Sadie, darling, be a love and make another cup of tea, would you?"

Standing up and grabbing the teapot, I heard myself make a tiny sniffing noise, same as Gran had done. Mine could be translated as, "Actually, in principle, I don't mind making *Mum* a cup of tea, but I don't see why I should have to do it this time since a) I don't drink the stuff, and b) I'm tired after a hard day's maths, geography, physics, etc., while YOU have only been swanning about, going to the wrong art gallery, so why don't YOU make it, Nonna?!"

I don't think Nonna picked up any of that from the sniff.

"Are you all right, Nicola, darling? You're looking a bit tired and drawn. Positively pale," said Nonna, sounding concerned as she studied Mum's perfectly normal, perfectly pleasant face.

"I'm fine," replied Mum, jiggling a cooing Martha in her arms. She didn't look tired or drawn or pale to me. Just a tiny bit tense, maybe.

"Are you *sure*, Nicola? You look a bit sickly. Not your best."

Ah, Tactless Nonna was stomping all over Mum's confidence really nicely.

Mum responded by ignoring Nonna altogether. I think if anything was wrong with her, it was a case of Wound-Up-By-Critical-Mother-ness (no known cure, sadly).

"Sadie, Sonny – your dad texted me at work to ask if it would be all right to go to tea at his tomorrow instead of tonight, 'cause he's got to work late to get an order out."

"Fine by me," I shrugged, as I filled the kettle.

"Can't do it tomorrow – got rehearsals," I heard Sonny say.

"And I won't be there, either," said Gran, reappearing in the room and immediately multitasking by patting Mum a warm hello on the back, pulling the buttons of Martha's cardie out of her mouth, and swiping the kettle from me. (Yay.) "I've promised to go and see my friend Barbara – she's in hospital with her gall bladder. It's fit to burst, she says, so they've got to whip it out!"

Released from my tea-making duty, I turned around and spied Nonna making a retching face to Sonny. I guess she was just trying to be funny, but I wished it wasn't at Gran's expense. I mean, straight or not, Gran was here for us all three-hundred-and-sixty-five days of the year, while we only saw Nonna once in a blue moon. Or when the builders were in her Spanish flat, of course.

"But I'll leave you and your dad a little something for your tea before I go out, Sadie!" Gran promised, hauling on some yellow rubber gloves and getting ready to do some dishes in the ten seconds it would take for the kettle to boil.

"But surely Martin could make his *own* meal for himself and his daughter!" laughed Nonna. "After all, he *is* a grown man!!"

Gran stopped mid-scrub, her shoulders hunched and rigid. "It's *Max*," she growled.

"Yes, of course, of course," said Nonna, waving

away Gran's words. "But you know, you really are spoiling him, Joan, living in his flat like an unpaid housekeeper!"

Gran was peeling off her rubber gloves, snapping each finger as she thought of a smart response. Or maybe she was just imagining snapping Nonna's *head* like that.

Uh-oh.

Another verbal boxing match was on the horizon. Mum had tensed up; I could tell because Martha was whingeing and struggling to get out of the grip that had turned from a lovely mummy snuggle to a stressed clench.

Y'know, Will had been reading a lot of childcare books lately, 'cause Martha was his first baby. And after school, he'd often tell me chunks of interesting facts, which, to be honest, weren't *that* interesting, but Will was so dopily devoted to Martha that I tended to half-listen and say stuff like "Is that right?" now and again just to keep him happy.

Suddenly now, I remembered something he'd read out about toddlers having tantrums. The minute you sense one starting, you're supposed to distract them. It's like, there they are, about to howl, and you go, "Hey! Look at this shiny toy!" and they're immediately hooked on it and forget to yell their lungs out.

Well, I figured a shiny toy was what we needed now, to avoid the next round of the Granny Wars.

And I knew my brother was the closest thing I had to a shiny toy. . .

"Hey, Sonny!" I said brightly. "That new song you're doing as a single. Have you figured out a dance routine for it?"

Maybe Sonny just wanted to show off (he doesn't usually *get* anything subtle), but I like to think that for once, he was acting like a proper psychic twin and reading my mind.

"Uh, yeah!" he said, sticking the Jaffa Cakes back on the table and getting to his feet. "You want to see?"

No would be the normal, sensible answer, but of course, that wasn't the correct response at a difficult time like this.

"Yes!" I said, hoping I sounded for real, as Sonny fished a CD from his school bag and put it in the player on the shelf above the dishwasher.

"Oooh, yes, please!" both our grans chorused, in matching delight.

It's a very cringeworthy and bizarre thing, having your brother pull some seriously corny dance moves round your kitchen, but it did the trick.

With sniping instantly forgotten (or at least put aside), Gran and Nonna watched, transfixed. Actually, they reminded me of Dog when you waft a slice of ham in front of her feline face.

Whatever; hurray for the shiny-toy trick.

Crisis averted.

Granny Wars postponed.

I deserved a medal.

(Especially for having to listen to that *awful* single twice in the space of a week. . .)

9

Rants, moans and sandwiches

"Are you expecting a troupe of scouts?" I asked Dad.

"Don't be silly, Sadie," he said, standing beside me with his hands in his jeans' pockets, wearing his favourite, very *loud* Hawaiian shirt. "The entire cast of the *Lion King* musical said they might pop round for a snack after their show is over tonight."

We were staring at the mountain of sandwiches Gran had left for us on a silver platter on the kitchen worktop, cling film straining over the top of the pile.

"Has she thought of a career in catering?" asked Cormac, peering round the doorframe into the kitchen, for once in his off-duty uniform of jeans and T-shirt. "My dad could hire her to do the catering for our funerals!"

With Sonny so busy with his career, Cormac was fast feeling like an alternative brother, and not just a mate. A "brother" that I maybe had a bit more in common with than the real one I once shared nine months in a womb with.

"Do you want to hire my *other* gran?" I asked him, stepping towards the Mount Kilimanjaro of egg, ham and cheese sandwiches. "Nonna would be great at helping bereaved people get over their loss."

"How?" asked Cormac, as Dad handed him a paper plate with Rory the Racing Car on (he obviously couldn't be bothered with any washing up tonight).

"Well, she'd just be so *annoying* that they'd forget to be upset, and want to kill her instead!"

Yes, I was very cross with Nonna; *no*, I hadn't seen much of her funny or nice sides for a couple of days.

"Is she driving you nuts, then?" asked Cormac, helping himself to a handful of daintily cut bread.

"She kept herself very busy today," I said darkly. "By rearranging my *bedroom*. . ."

I wanted to rearrange an earlier flight back to *Spain* when I saw that.

"Uh-oh; I'm guessing that you didn't know that was going to happen?" Cormac mumbled sympathetically, with a full mouth.

"Nope, I didn't know."

I didn't know that the bed would "look better" against the opposite wall, I didn't know my desk would "get more light" if it was by the wardrobe, and I certainly didn't know that the shelves I had stacked with all my stuff would be improved by pinning a throw to the front "to hide all the clutter".

I had the thrill of finding all that out when I got home from school today.

And Nonna explained it to me when I went upstairs and caught her rifling through my wardrobe, pulling out anything she thought was a better option than the clothes I usually wore.

"Now *this*," she said, holding out a frilly, lilac-y shirt that my Aunt Diane sent me as a present, and which was *so* not me. "*This* would be just lovely with something like a cute little fuchsia, swirly skirt!"

Yes, it might. But the idea of me wearing a cute little fuchsia, swirly skirt was as funny as the idea of Clyde dressing as a nun.

"I really *must* take you shopping on Saturday!" said Generous Nonna, who seemed oblivious to the fact that Tactless and Mad Nonna had come *that* close to being murdered just now. (I could see the headlines: "Teen Strangles Gran With Frilly Shirt".)

"Can't – got something to do on Saturday," I mumbled, stomping downstairs without a clue in my head about what I was going to be doing two days from now. "Anyway, I'm going back out now – got to meet Dad from work!"

Apart from Nonna, no one else was in the house, so I had no one to rant to. Mum and Sonny weren't back from work and school yet, though I didn't suppose I could safely rant to Mum about Nonna anyway, and Sonny was someone I generally ranted *at*, not *to*. As for Will and Martha, it was Thursday, so they'd be on their way back from some baby music class they attended together, where the parents sang "Wheels On The Bus" and the babies tried to eat the tambourines.

And Gran? Well, after the last subtle sniping session, I suspected that she'd *definitely* be boycotting our house till Nonna was safely back in Spain. In fact, I bet Gran would be raising a glass of sherry and waving a flag in celebration as Nonna's plane headed into the clouds. . .

So off I'd headed to Bird's Paper Products, which was five minutes' walk (two minutes when you were speed-walking through fury) from our house.

Of course, Dad wasn't expecting me so early. I'd like to say I found him hard at work, stacking piles of Disney Princess serviettes or whatever, but instead I heard him and his work buddies yelling along to Queen's "Bohemian Rhapsody" on the radio from halfway along the street. At least Daryl and Kemal had the decency to look embarrassed at being caught warbling the operatic high bits – Dad just kept right on singing, directly to me, when he saw me standing in the open doorway, arms across my chest, my eyes narrowed at him.

Anyway, Dad took my appearance as a good excuse to finish up early, and off we'd wandered, back to his flat, where he immediately put an old Jam album on at full volume, and started singing along as he pulled open the door on to the fire escape.

RAT-A-TAT-TAT!!, he'd hammered on the metal handrail (secret code to Cormac in the flat upstairs for "Come down if you fancy!").

And so Cormac *had* come down, and luckily hadn't had his tea, and so could help us dispose of a fraction of Gran's latest mega-snack.

"Are you still doing a stand-up session on Sunday morning?" I asked Cormac, wandering back into the living room with my seventeen sandwiches.

"Yep, and my mates have all said they'll come," said Cormac, spluttering a bit as he choked on a ham 'n' mustard on wheatgerm.

"Great. But I'm guessing I *shouldn't* invite Nonna, right?" I said, shooting him a knowing look; i.e., knowing that he'd be taking the mick out of her especially.

"Probably not. . ." Cormac shot a sheepish look at Dad, as if taking the mick out of his ex-mother-in-law was maybe a little out of order.

"Hey, don't mind me!" said Dad, parking himself in his favourite tan leather armchair. "Muriel's driven me mad enough over the years! Oh, but I've just remembered something! *I* know a story about her that you should use!"

Me and Cormac both perked up, keen to hear what he had to say.

"Yeah . . . I can't remember the exact details," Dad mused, unaware of the bit of lettuce dangling from his chin like a tiny green goatee, "but the gist of it is that she once ran away from home – but came back only to find no one noticed that she'd gone! Can't remember more than that. You'll have to ask your mum, Sadie."

A couple of hours later, and I was just about to. . .

10

I love you, *but*. . .

Home, sweet home. (Ha!)

Martha had gone off to Snoozeland ages ago, Sonny was either up in his room or not back yet from rehearsals, and Will and Nonna were in the living room peering at the titchy telly.

There was no sign of Mum, but there *was* a lot of clattering going on in the kitchen, as well as Classic FM blasting from the radio.

"What are you doing?"

Weird. Mum was on her hands and knees, pulling pots and pans out of the cupboard, with a bottle of spray detergent and a scrubbing sponge at her side.

"Just thought I'd give these cupboards a freshen up."

Weirder. I mean, Mum did *some* of the housework, but really it was Will – with his mild form of obsessive-compulsive disorder – who liked to do stuff like clean kitchen cupboards and polish plugs or whatever.

So what was Mum up to? I got down on my haunches beside her, readying myself to hit her with a tricky question. I was a little bit nervous, since we hadn't had this sort of conversation before, but felt I might as well just say it anyway.

"Mum . . . are you, um, doing this as an excuse to get away from Nonna?" I whispered.

Mum frowned at me.

Uh-oh – I'd said something too harsh for her. *She doesn't like anyone criticizing her mother*, I reminded myself.

Then Mum did a funny thing: she sighed and flopped down on to her bottom, as if she'd suddenly deflated.

"*Yes!*" she said, heaving a great sigh of relief. "She's making us watch five episodes of a *A Place In The Sun* back to back on some channel and I can't take it any more!"

I knew the programme she meant. A smiley, tanned presenter took two know-it-alls to a sunny country to help them look for their dream house. The know-it-all couple wouldn't speak the language, and would get grumpy with the smiley, tanned presenter for not showing them beachside mansions with pools, when for their budget, they could really only afford a shack by the supermarket with a puddle outside the front door.

Mum rested her back against the open cupboard and pushed her dark, wavy hair out of her face. She seemed exhausted all of a sudden, as if an alien presence had sucked all the life force out of her. (The alien presence being a Martian race known as the Nonnas. Expect to see them on an episode of *Dr Who* soon.)

"Y'know, she moved all the furniture around in my bedroom today," I told her, flopping down on the cool tiled floor beside her.

"Yes, she said. I told her she shouldn't have, but she said you didn't seem to mind. Which I doubted," Mum sighed.

"I *did* mind. That's why I took off to Dad's early."

"I guessed that. Wish I'd gone there too!" Mum grinned weakly at me.

"What – and left poor Will and Martha?" I asked, getting a buzz from the fact that me and Mum were actually starting to talk about the problem with Nonna, even if it was via jokey remarks.

"Oh, no! I would've taken them too."

"And left Nonna on her *own* in the house? Wouldn't she wonder where we all were?"

"Well, *eventually*. I mean, she'd probably talk and talk and talk to herself for hours till she noticed none of us were there!"

"Yeah – not till Sonny came back from rehearsals and saw that we'd all escaped!"

We were giggling, me and Mum, and it felt good. Then I remembered something I'd been dying to ask. Not about what Dad told me – not yet – but about Nonna's threats yesterday morning, when she'd come down and found me sleeping on the cushions and crumbs by Dog's cage.

"Has Nonna spoken to you about Clyde or Dog yet?" I asked Mum.

Of course, I knew she *had* – I'd heard her bending Mum's ear when I came down after my shower yesterday morning, and had turned right around and gone back up to hide out in my room to avoid the conversation.

By the time I'd tiptoed back down, Mum had gone to work and Nonna was watching morning telly, and the subject of the pets seemed to be strangely closed.

"Yes." Mum nodded slowly. "She told me we had to keep Clyde outside and that we should move Dog and her cage out of the living room and into the garden shed."

"What? But Dog would be cold out there, and she'd miss us, and miss *Mist: Sheepdog Tales* on Five, and that's her favourite!" I gasped.

Dog and Martha seemed to share a lot of the

same tastes when it came to kiddy TV. Though Dog didn't like *The Tweenies* very much and tended to walk back and forth in her cage when they came on and sang their screechy songs. Hey, maybe it *wasn't* cage-related stress that Dog was suffering from – it was Tweenies overload. . .

"Don't worry," said Mum, putting her hand over mine. "I told her no *way* – it was *our* house and not hers and the animals were staying where they were."

I flipped my hand round so it was palm up and gave her hand a grateful squeeze.

Right on cue, Clyde hopped into the kitchen, gave us both a dismissive glance, and padded to his litter tray at the side of the washing machine.

Seeing him made me think – at a slightly sideways angle – of Dog. Dog in her cage, who hopefully would be set free from jail on Saturday, if the vet gave her the thumbs up. Hey – maybe we could have a Free From Jail party for her!

It could be corny and dumb and fun.

Balloons, crisps, cat crunchies, the lot . . . with all friends and family invited – which could include Cormac, since he was definitely classed as a good friend by now (as well as token big brother). At least that was *one* way he could get a glimpse of the force of nature that was Nonna – *and* he'd be in a crowd, so it would be safer.

If he could make it, that was. Maybe he'd be busy with all the dead people. . .

"Is she getting to you, honey?" asked Mum, slipping a comforting arm around my shoulders.

"She drives me *crazy*, Mum," I said, glad to get the words out at last.

"Trust me, honey, she drives *me* crazy too." Mum smiled at me.

Admitting it at last seemed amazing, a really special moment. And to match the mood, the violins on the radio in the background reached a crescendo and faded out, so all we could hear was the hissing of rabbit pee on litter.

"Why haven't you said so before?" I asked Mum.

"It's complicated."

"Complicated how?"

"Well, a lot of the time I feel . . . *sorry* for her, Sadie."

Wow. I felt lots of things about Nonna, depending on which version of her I was dealing with, but sorry was never one of them.

Mum saw that my brain was exploding with the word "Why?" and started to explain.

"She's just had a lot of disappointments in her life."

"Like?"

Finished with what he was doing, Clyde hopped on over to join us, as though me and Mum slouching on the floor by the cupboard under the sink, whispering together, was something he saw all the time.

"Well. . ." began Mum, with a sudden faraway look in her eyes, same as she gets when she's listening to a piece of classical music that she likes.

I gave her a gentle nudge with my elbow to bring her back from her brainly meanderings and get to the point.

"She *desperately* wanted to be an air stewardess when she was young, and travel the world, but her parents were pretty strict and thought it was unsuitable and pooh-poohed it. They made her go to secretarial college instead," said Mum, stroking Clyde's ears with her free hand.

Lucky us, I thought. Nonna's parents would be spinning in their graves (unless they'd been cremated) if they knew about Sonny's burning desire to sing, dance or act. And as well as encouraging *him*, I knew that Mum and Dad would support me and Martha in whatever we wanted to do for our careers. Though at the moment, I had as much idea about what I wanted to do as Martha. . .

"And then she married your granddad, and I think she thought it would be the time that her life would properly begin. But even though he was kind and lovely, he wasn't very dynamic. He didn't like travelling very much, and we only ever went on caravan holidays to places like Northumberland and Wales."

Northumberland and Wales were very nice, I was sure, but for someone who wanted to travel the world, I guess Swansea wasn't exactly Shanghai.

"But Nonna got to live in Spain eventually, though, didn't she?" I pointed out.

"Yes, but her second marriage didn't work out and her third husband died after only a few years, so . . . well. . ."

So, well, I sort of saw Mum's point. I did suddenly feel a pang for Nonna, even if all her disappointments didn't quite excuse her barging her larger-than-life personality all over the place, squashing people's feelings as she went.

Still. . .

"Oh, but Dad said something about Nonna once running away from home!" I said, remembering the start of the story again. "He said I should ask you about it."

"Ah, yes . . . that is quite a sad story." Mum nodded. "She *did* run away from home. She got it in her head that she wanted to see Paris. She got as far as the bus station in Victoria, then chickened out and came home. But no one realized she was gone in the first place!"

"How could no one notice? How old was she?" I frowned, worried for the small girl – aching to see the world – who was my now bossy, overbearing Nonna.

"She was thirty-four," said Mum thoughtfully, not seeming to be aware of how, well, *funny* that sounded.

"Thirty-four?!" I repeated. "Can people still run away from home when they're thirty-four?"

I *had* to tell Cormac about this. It was perfect for his routine for Sunday.

"Well, *she* did. And because my dad had been at work and I was at school, we didn't find out till she burst into tears and told us over tea that night."

OK, now I felt *properly* sorry for Nonna. I didn't think I'd be sharing this particular story with Cormac after all.

"That is quite sad," I said softly.

"Yes, it is," Mum agreed.

We were quiet for a bit, apart from the screechy choral music on the radio (which was starting to do my head in). And in that quiet(ish) moment, I realized how lucky I was to have the parents I did, even if they weren't together.

"Y'know, Nonna *can* be really nice."

"Yes, she can."

"And funny and kind, when she wants to be."

"Yes, that too," acknowledged Mum, with a soft squeeze of my shoulder.

"Oh! Hello! What are you two doing down there?" asked Nonna, suddenly appearing in the kitchen doorway.

"I was just telling Sadie how much I love you," Mum said, smiling at Nonna and giving my shoulder a tiny squeeze.

I knew how to translate that. It meant: "I love her, *but*. . ."

"Oh, how sweet of you, darling!" sighed Nonna, looking a little teary-eyed and blowing Mum a kiss. "And I love you too!"

It was a nice moment – even if it was perfumed by the germ-killing spray cleaner Mum had just been using.

"So . . ." Nonna began, "who's going to get the kettle on and make me a nice cup of tea!"

Hmmm. Was that Funny Nonna, teasing us, or Tactless Nonna expecting waitress service?

Who knows; sometimes the Nonnas blurred together.

"How much longer is she staying?" I whispered, as we heard Nonna stamp up the stairs.

Mum checked her watch.

"Six days, eight hours and fifty minutes," she whispered back. "Not that I'm counting. . ."

Oops, I broke the cat

Snippp!!

"*I'll* take those, thank you!" said the vet, scooping a pair of small scissors out of Harry's hand.

"Harry! I said DON'T TOUCH ANYTHING!!" Hannah hissed at her brother, who'd just cut a chunk of the front of his hair with the scissors he'd helped himself to from the instrument tray.

When Hannah phoned me earlier and asked if we could hang out, I told her that was fine, except it would have to involve hanging out at the vet's, since that's where I had to take Dog this Saturday morning.

She didn't tell me at that point that she'd been left to look after Harry, mainly because she hadn't (been left to look after him, I mean). Her parents had set up a play-date for her weaselly brother while her dad was playing golf and her mum was at the hairdresser. Once everyone had left, Hannah had been looking forward to a chilled-out stretch on the sofa with only the TV for company before she came to hang out with me. Then *bing-bong* went the doorbell, and Harry was delivered back from his play-date an hour and a half early due to using toothpaste to create a punk, Mohican hairstyle on his friend's startled hamster, after he was specifically told not to go near it.

Naturally, Hannah hadn't bothered to phone me and tell me she was bringing Harry along with her, because she knew I'd flee the country. . .

Hannah was now holding Harry's arms pinned to his sides, while her eyes scanned the room, spotting the array of lethal syringes and pet medicines that the Weasel might try and get his hands on when no one was looking.

Hey, maybe me and Hannah should have chipped in together and bought a lead and a muzzle for him while we were here.

Snippp!!

"There!" said the vet, putting down the scissors and swiftly pulling the last chunk of black stitch out. "Cruciate ligament fixed!"

The vet was talking directly to Dog, as if she could understand. But Dog didn't understand *anything* apart from the fact that someone was fiddling around doing something uncomfortable to her shaved back leg and she didn't like it very much.

"Hissssssssss!"

"All done!" said the vet, waggling the fur on the top of Dog's head, totally unperturbed by the hissing. But I guess when you're used to dealing with snarly pit bulls and poisonous snakes, a hissy cat isn't going to worry you too much.

"Thank you, " I said, lifting the cat basket up off the floor so Dog could scoot inside. (Funny how cats can forcibly wedge themselves into the back of the cat basket when you need them to come out, and can then effortlessly disappear into it like a magician's trick when it's time to go.)

"Oooh, I see from your computer file that Dog's used up rather a lot of her nine lives!" said the vet, staring at the screen as I struggled with one of the two snibs that locked the basket. Dog stared closely at my stumbling fingers. Any second now, she'd be tap-tap-tapping her claws impatiently, desperate for me to get on with it.

"Yep," I replied. I didn't need to look at the computer screen to see how long the list of visits to the vet's was. Since we'd had her, Dog had managed to fall off, get stuck under, and be hit by a whole ton of stuff, as well as catch every serious cat bug going. I think she may well have used up something closer to thirty-two lives.

Whatever, I didn't say more than "yep", because the vet pointed it out every time we came here. Which, as you can gather, was quite a lot.

Instead, I just thought about the Free From Jail party we were going to throw for Dog this afternoon. The one Harry was most definitely *not* invited to. Will was outside in the waiting room with Martha, making a mental list of shopping we'd need to pick up if Dog got the green light to be uncaged, which she absolutely, definitely, joyously had.

Bring on the Kettle Chips. . .

"*I* can do that!" said Harry, wriggling free from Hannah's restraining arms.

"*Leave* it, Harry!" warned his sister.

"Harry – don't!" I ordered him.

But in a split second, he managed to fidget the snibs of the basket open.

Ping!

"Can I come to your cat party now?" asked Harry, hopefully.

"Nope," I told him, watching as the vet gave Dog a last scratch of the head.

"Well, I hope you try and keep good care of this little hissy miss from now on!" the vet joked kindly to me.

"Absolutely," I assured him, as I watched Dog glide her way into the basket.

"*Yeeeeooooooww!*" yelped Dog, as I slammed the wire door shut *right* on her tail.

"Ha ha ha ha ha ha ha ha ha ha!" laughed the Weasel.

Now *how* much was that muzzle. . .?

I love those rare times when Letty and Hannah forget to be bugged by each other's presence and just have a laugh.

They were having a laugh together right now. At my expense. (Glad I'm useful for *something*. . .)

"You *didn't*!" sniggered Letty, slapping her hand across her mouth a couple of hours later, when I told her what had happened.

"She *did*!" grinned Hannah.

"*And* we had to pay for another X-ray, just to make sure it wasn't broken!" added Will, passing us with a tray of sausage rolls straight from the oven and catching the tail end of the conversation. (Oh, how appropriate. . .)

"Hey – you know what wasn't fair? Sadie didn't even get into trouble, and *I* got into so much trouble this morning at my friend's house, and I was only using toothpaste!!" Harry chipped in, hovering suddenly close to me, his voice buzzing in my head like a bluebottle fly.

"Yeah, toothpaste and a defenceless *hamster*. . ." I muttered to Letty, wishing Harry wasn't here. I silently cursed the lack of mobile reception on the golf course Hannah's dad was playing on, as well as the hairdresser who'd accidentally turned Hannah's mum's hair luminous orange instead of luscious honey, causing her to sit for another couple of hours in the salon while it got fixed.

("I can't look after him on my own, Sadie!!" Hannah had appealed to my sympathetic side, after she took the call from her mum while Dog was in getting her X-ray. It was true – a person on their own would need to have a lasso or a taser gun to keep Harry under control, so he'd ended up at the Free From Jail party after all.)

"Wait – so you got your cat fixed, then you practically *broke* her straightaway?!" said Cormac ten minutes later, when I had to tell the whole story again.

"Yeah, but look – she's OK, isn't she?" I said, pointing down to Dog, who was rolling luxuriously on her back on the fluffy carpet in the middle of the living room.

Dad and Cormac had just turned up, looking like a bizarre double act: Dad in long, baggy shorts, pale blue Hawaiian shirt (his second favourite) and long sandy-coloured sideburns, while Cormac was in his black suit, since someone had carelessly gone and died this morning, which was rather selfish of them when Cormac had a cat party to go to.

"Have you invited half of Highbury to come, then, Sadie?" asked Dad, nodding at the banquet spread out on the table that had been dragged through from the kitchen.

Gran had temporarily given up on her boycott of our house (again) as soon as she knew her catering skills were required.

Though she wasn't the only one in our family to get into the party spirit – Will hadn't just bought the food, he'd decorated the living room too, with rows of balloons pinned up on the walls (at the same height, equally spaced, and in rigidly alternating colours of orange, green and blue). Bless him; he'd even kept Harry out of mischief pre-party by ordering him to blow them all up, handing them back if they weren't inflated to exactly the same size.

Mum had done the music (i.e., put on a CD of light classical operettas which I'd have loved to change to something rockier, only it would've sent Dog scurrying to her cat flap).

And Nonna . . . Nonna had slipped on her gold sandals and was wearing a loose, floaty shirt that looked a deep coral in some lights and a dark amber in others.

"I just love parties!" she'd said, when I told her earlier that she looked nice. "Though having one for a cat does seem rather *silly*, doesn't it?"

Grrrr. . . Why couldn't she just go with the flow and say nothing about the silliness (which was part of the fun, after all)? I mean, I knew sensible, straight Gran thought it was silly too, but she was thrilled to have any excuse for a family get-together.

Yikes – speaking of Nonna, here she came right now. . .

"Sadie, darling; what's the name of that horrible little boy again?" she asked bluntly.

"*Harry*," said Gran, swooping by with a platter of mini-pizzas at that moment and answering Nonna's question for me. The way she said his name, you'd think she'd just caught a whiff of cowpat.

"Well, Joan, I just found Harry in the kitchen cramming three of your home-made jam tarts in his mouth at once," said Nonna. "I made him spit them out in the bin."

That sounded kind of extreme, but hey, Harry deserved it.

"Why, that little. . ." Gran mumbled, storming off towards the kitchen.

"Don't worry – I told his sister and she's got him under house arrest!" Nonna joked over her shoulder at Gran.

"Well, we've still got Dog's cage going spare, remember!" Gran joked back as she disappeared out of the room.

Wow. Maybe the Weasel had his uses after all. Nonna and Gran had – miracle of miracles – almost bonded there over their mutual dislike of him. Yay!

"Anyway, enough of obnoxious little boys," said Nonna smoothly, turning her attention to Cormac and holding an elegant hand out to him. "You must be Cormac! I'm Sadie and Sonny's nonna!"

"It's Italian," Letty said usefully, hovering by Cormac's elbow. "For grandmother."

I saw Nonna flinch a little. Even after all these years, she still seemed to struggle with the word. I should remember to use that as a weapon against her next time she was driving me crazy.

"Cormac, call me Bunny, *please* – everyone does," said Nonna, throwing out an arm to the room, which was filled with people who generally *didn't* call her Bunny.

"Um, OK . . . *Bunny*. . .!" said Cormac, turning

a bit pink in her forceful presence. Or maybe it was because she'd taken one of his hands in both of hers and was staring intently at him.

"And you're the boy who works at the funeral director's," she said, patting with the hand that was on top of his.

"Uh, yes," Cormac confirmed.

Out of the corner of my eye, I could see Hannah now shoving Harry on to the floor in front of our tiddly TV with a bowlful of Hula Hoops, switching it on to some random rubbish channel, and ordering him to stay there, much like you'd do to a dog outside a shop. Pity she couldn't legally tie him up.

Then – spotting Nonna on full charm offensive with Cormac – Hannah came scuttling over to listen in.

Dad was listening intently too, doing his best to hide his smirks by taking a big bite of one of the five quiches Gran had made.

"It's a very, very noble profession to work in," Nonna said earnestly.

"Well, thank you," Cormac replied, with the sort of courteous nod he must give to his clients (the relatives, I mean, not the *dead* people).

"It's *such* a sensitive area, and it must be *very* rewarding," Nonna continued.

"It's certainly a privilege to help make the end of someone's life a special time," said Cormac, sounding like he was quoting from *The Good Undertaker's Manual*, but I knew he really meant it.

"Yes, indeed." Nonna nodded with a sincere expression. "I suppose it must also be a . . . a . . ."

Nonna hesitated, her brow furrowed. Me, Cormac, Letty, Hannah and Dad waited with bated breath.

Nonna lost her frown of concentration and smiled brightly as she found the words she was looking for.

". . . a little *dreary*?"

Dad immediately began to choke and splutter on a mouthful of quiche. Tactless Nonna turned quickly to administer a helpful pat on the back, which gave me, Cormac, Letty and Hannah a chance to hide our sniggers and try to pull ourselves together.

"I haven't missed much, have I?" Sonny's voice suddenly cut across the music and choking going on in the room. He was standing in the doorway, glancing around.

"You haven't missed much of the *party*." I grinned over at him, wishing I could tell him he *had* missed Nonna cheerfully insulting Cormac.

But she was still close at hand, irritatedly waving away the glass of water Gran had appeared with and was holding out, and making Dad bend right over by suddenly pressing her hand very firmly on his neck. (Dad seemed to be shaking a lot. I wasn't sure if that was because he was laughing or because he was still choking.)

"What's with Dad?" Sonny asked, dropping his bag and jacket on to the sofa.

"Got attacked by quiche," I explained, suddenly noticing two things:

1) Gran looking hurt at being waved away by Nonna, and 2) Will quickly distracting Gran by filling her sherry glass to the brim.

So much for the Harry-induced truce between her and Nonna. . .

"Oh. Are you OK?" asked Sonny, going down on his haunches to chat to Dad.

"Uh-huh," Dad grunted in reply, as Nonna thumped him heartily on the back.

Seeming reassured, Sonny straightened up and carried on chatting to me.

"Anyway, glad I'm here on time – I got out of rehearsal early specially," said Sonny, suddenly spotting the reason for the party. "Hey, hello, Dog!! Wow, look at you, with no cage cooping you up!"

He took a couple of steps forward and went down on his haunches again – this time to rub Dog's tummy.

Guilt: that's what it must have been, since he'd caused Dog's injury in the first place.

Still, he was here. We were *all* here. As soon as Dad stopped choking, we needed to get on with this dumb party for Dog before she got restless and felt like going on a patrol of the garden. That's if Dad didn't need the Heimlich manoeuvre or to be taken to A&E or something.

"Hey, look! I'm fine, I'm fine!" Dad announced, at that moment standing upright and holding his hand out for the medicinal beer that Will was now offering him.

Out of the corner of my eye (again), I spotted our titchy TV – with no one stuck in front of it. Where was the Weasel? What hideous bad behaviour or practical jokes was he planning now? It was like having a python let loose at a duckling's birthday party. . .

Oh – panic over. Harry was just at the table, trying to fit three bowlfuls' worth of food into his one Hula Hoops bowl. It was greedy, rude and stupid, but I could handle that.

"TA-NA!!"

A voice trilling from the doorway. Mum's.

She was holding a cake – a home-made cake in the shape of. . .

"What's it supposed to be?" Cormac whispered in my ear.

"A litter tray!" I hissed back.

Yep, it was a red icing litter tray with bumpy grey icing inside for the granules of litter. It had nine lit candles sticking in it.

"Is it your cat's birthday?" asked Cormac, forgetting to whisper.

"It's for her nine lives," Dad answered him.

"Sadie and Sonny's gran made this – I thought I'd better say that before *I* get the credit!" said Mum, placing the cake down on the table. Harry's eyes lit up at the sight of all that icing. He'd better keep his paws off till he was offered a bit (what were the chances of *that* happening?).

"*And* Martha's. Martha's gran too," Gran added softly, gazing adoringly at my chubby little sister, snuggled in Will's arms.

"And Martha's granny too, of *course*," said Will, passing her over to Gran.

Nonna immediately went to add something.

"Yes, well," she began, "but, *technically*, Joan isn't—"

Nooooo!!! I thought in a fleeting second, as Tactless Nonna opened her mouth to state the obvious.

I mean, *yes*, so Gran was *Dad's* mum, so no, technically she *wasn't* Martha's biological grandmother, but they loved each other madly and Gran got upset if anyone pointed out that Martha wasn't every bit her beloved grandchild, same as me and Sonny.

Tactless Nonna *had* to be stopped!! Where was an electric cattle prod when you needed one?! Maybe I should just pick Harry up and throw him at her (he wasn't much use for anything else).

"HAPPY FREEDOM TO YOOOOUU!!!" Sonny suddenly boomed out in his best coached singing voice, completely obliterating what Nonna was about to blurt.

He stood up, lifting Dog with him, and walked over to the table, the cake and the lit candles, waving an arm at everyone to join in to the tune of "Happy Birthday".

"HAPPY FREEDOM TO YOOOOUU!!!"

Did Sonny just decide to do that goofy, made-up song because it suited the dumb party? Or had he deliberately tried to avert the Granny Wars kicking off again? Could he *be* that thoughtful and smart? Well, there's always a first time. . .

"HAPPY FREEDOM, DEAR DOOOOGGG!!" everyone in the room sang along to humour him. Including Nonna, who might have thought the party

was silly, but did anything Sonny asked her to. And including Harry, who I noticed was trying to stuff a handful of sausage rolls down his trousers to save for later (hurrah – at least he wasn't squirting shaving foam on the jam tarts).

"HAPPY FREEDOM TO YOOOOOOOUUU!!"

Well, whether he'd meant to or not, Sonny had Done A Good Thing.

Oh . . . except for *that* thing.

There – where he swung around with Dog tucked under his arm; where Dog's tail swished into the candles on the litter-tray cake; where the candles landed on the *Aristocats* paper tablecloth that had been Dad's contribution to the party.

Yes, *that*.

Setting the house on fire during a cat party was most definitely A Not-Good Thing.

"Ha ha ha ha ha ha ha ha ha – hic!!" chortled Harry the Weasel, almost (hopefully) choking on his sixty-seventh sausage roll. . .

Added nuts

". . .and *that*, ladies and gentlemen, is why you should never, *EVER* have a party for a cat."

The crowd of about thirty people (and several dogs) whooped and clapped (well, maybe not the dogs) as Cormac came to the end of his routine in Highbury Fields park this Sunday morning.

"Wow . . . Cormac was brilliant, wasn't he?" Letty sighed as the clapping and the whooping went on.

I wasn't looking, but I bet Hannah was rolling her eyes. She had about as much patience for Letty's loser crushes as I had for Sonny's spontaneous tap-dancing routines. Luckily, only *I* usually spotted the eye-rolling stuff, but dippy as she might be, it was only a matter of time before Letty clocked on. Please just let it be a *long* time. My weird triangular friendship was hard enough to deal with without a row.

"Yes, he was," I said truthfully, feeling the sort

of ripple of pride for Cormac that I would have had for Sonny, if his band had been good and not useless.

"Oh. . ." muttered Letty, slightly crestfallen. "Where's he going?"

She'd been expecting Cormac to step off his microscopic stage (an upturned wooden crate) and come straight over to us for some post-performance chat. I guess I had too.

Instead he'd bounded down and weaved through the entertained dog walkers to someone – or a *few* someones – just behind us to the left.

"Hey, they must be his friends!" said Hannah, as we all watched him walk up to four lads dressed in more or less matching outfits of baggy trousers and football tops.

"I saw them earlier," I murmured, remembering when I snuck a look round – OK, *lots* of looks round – to suss how Cormac's routine was going down. I'd seen plenty of grinning faces, except for those particular four lads at the back in Arsenal shirts. It's not that they hadn't been laughing, exactly; they'd been sniggering together for sure, but in that way people do when they're taking the mick.

I hadn't realized those were Cormac's *mates*. . .

"They *can't* be his friends – they're not really

smiling properly at him," Letty said protectively, as the three of us girls checked out the ongoing body language between Cormac and the four lads.

And the body language read like this: Cormac grinning at first, though his grin was dimming as they chatted – the boys' arms were folded or they had hands shoved in pockets, with faces guarded and smug.

It was pretty obvious: they were *embarrassed* by him, and Cormac was *just* getting the message loud and clear. . .

"Hey, look!" Dad's voice came from beside us. "Cormac's pointing us out to those lads he's with!"

So he was. Dad gave Cormac an encouraging wave. So did Letty, only it was a bit less encouraging and more floppy and lovelorn.

The four boys didn't seem too impressed.

Cormac seemed to be trying to motion to them to come over and meet us, but there were a few "well-I-dunno" head shakes and shoulder shrugs going on. Which to me – non-professor of body language that I was – meant they weren't planning on coming anywhere near us if they could possibly help it. They had much better, laddish things to do, like kicking stones along the pavement or practising looking bored.

"Where are they going?" asked Sonny, watching as the four lads now started retreating, giving half-hearted waves in Cormac's direction before sloping off.

"Away," I said matter-of-factly. I was too busy watching Cormac to speculate. He was coming back towards us through his dispersing audience, giving the feeblest smiles to anyone doing a thumbs up to him (and plenty were).

He looked crushed.

"Hey, did your friends like your show?" twittered Letty, her head too stuffed with fluffy loveness to properly think that question through and match it to what we just saw happening.

"They never really said," muttered Cormac, completely thrown by their rejection, it was pretty easy to see.

"Were you trying to get them to come over or something?" Sonny asked him next.

Duh. Hey, Cormac was *hardly* asking them if they fancied joining him in doing a dance routine to *High School Musical*, was he? At least I could put Letty's no-brainer question down to dumbness-due-to-infatuation, but Sonny had *no* excuse. He was just a nerk.

"I'd mentioned you guys to them before," said Cormac, with a shrug of his shoulders. "Thought they might wanna, y'know, come over and meet you or whatever. But hey. . ."

OK – *I* got it.

According to Cormac, his old school buddies already thought it was seriously weird that he'd gone into the family firm (i.e., an undertaker's). Now that they'd seen his comedy routine, they thought it was weird, not to mention embarrassing, that their old mate wanted to stand in the middle of the park, making a fool of himself (while wearing his best funeral suit).

Best of all (worst of all?), their old mate was trying to introduce them to his *new* friends. *Us*. I could see how "us" looked to that bunch of seventeen-year-old boys. Three thirteen-year-old schoolgirls, a stage-school brat who was in a junior boy band, and a forty-something-year-old bloke with sandy-coloured Elvis sideburns and a bad-taste Hawaiian shirt.

Actually, that last bit was pretty funny, I decided. It was almost something Cormac could use in one of his routines. But I didn't say that out loud – not with the current, crushed version of Cormac standing in front of me.

With his spiky red hair and goofy expression, he usually looked pretty comical in his funeral suit, like a character that might turn up in an episode of *The Simpsons*.

But right now, for the first time since I'd got to know Cormac, his expression actually *matched* his funeral suit. . .

Wasps are not toys

It's amazing what can happen in the space of a quick trip to the loo.

When I nipped upstairs, Gran had been outside in the garden with a giggling Martha, making daisy chains that Dog was trying to play with. (Even with Nonna around, Gran couldn't keep away from Martha for too long or she got the shakes.)

Will had been on the phone, hassling the electrical store that had promised faithfully to get us a new cable for the big telly and hadn't.

Nonna was on her mobile, shouting in Spanish at someone who I supposed was her builder again. (*Please* don't let it have been about the work over-running – I needed my room back on Thursday, or I might just die from snore-induced sleep deprivation.)

And Letitia was at the kitchen table, flicking though a copy of some magazine she'd bought on the walk to my house from school. (It was

Monday, and the first day that Sonny's band had done one of their school showcases – she was dying to know how it went.)

Anyway, "I'll just be a minute" – that's what I'd said to Letty as I headed upstairs.

Well, a lot can happen in a minute.

When I came back down, Dog was still outside, trying to pounce on wasps now. (Eight weeks stuck in a cage and she'd forgotten the drawback of wasps as toys. She'd remember soon enough.)

Gran had a wailing Martha plonked on the draining board by the sink, and was picking earth out of her mouth and gently telling her off for eating bits of the garden.

Will had begun sanding down the kitchen table, in an attempt to get rid of the charred patch where the paper tablecloth had burned before Gran did her fire-fighter act on Saturday and extinguished the flames with a pitcher of orange juice.

So where was Letty? Not where I left her.

"She's through there with Bunny," said Will, nodding in the direction of the living room.

And sure enough, there they were, Nonna and Letty, deep in conversation on the sofa. Call me nosy (yeah, well, isn't *everyone*), but I hesitated outside the doorway so I could listen in for a second and see what strange subject they'd bonded over.

"Honestly, they were being so *mean* to him! Sort of sniggering, you know what I mean?"

"Tsk, tsk," tutted Nonna, with a shake of her elegantly styled silvery-blonde hair. "Well, it certainly couldn't have been nice for Cormac. But I suppose friendships do move on, and some wither by the wayside, as Shakespeare once said, if I remember rightly. . ."

Bet she *wasn't* remembering rightly, and I bet Shakespeare didn't say anything of the kind. It was probably a line Nonna half-remembered from a historical romance novel she'd once read.

But whatever; Letty was telling her about Cormac and his less-than-supportive mates, then?

"Ooh, but I was so *angry*! I felt like following them and telling them off!"

Through the space in the door, I saw Letty clutch her fists and Nonna pat my friend's knee.

"You've got a real crush on young Cormac, haven't you, Letitia, my little wildflower?"

Her name means "JOY"! I shouted in my head.

"Yes!" Letty gasped, surprised that it had been so obvious. "But no one knows – except Sadie! *And* Hannah, I'm pretty sure. . ."

Her face darkened a little as she said Hannah's name. Better have a word with Hannah now about all that unsubtle eye-rolling in Letty's – and

Cormac's – presence, if I wanted to avoid future friend-hassle. It was enough dealing with feuding grannies.

"Don't worry," Nonna reassured her. "Your secret's safe with me, Letitia, dear. I know you might think I'm past it now, but I had plenty of crushes on people when I was younger!"

Now you see? *That's* how confusing Nonna could be – as subtle as a sledgehammer one day (specially Saturday, when she nearly blurted out the biological grandma line) and sweet and kind as a fairy godmother the next. It did my head in.

But I couldn't hover out here all day. I supposed I'd better go in there and join the Fantasy Boyfriend conversation. . .

"Hi!" yelled Sonny, bursting my eardrums at the same time as he burst through the front door.

Urgh . . . he was still in full stage gear – the luminous purple and black cycling shorts, black T-shirt, baseball cap and make-up. Not eyeshadow or anything bizarre, but orange-y foundation and (I'm pretty sure) some mascara.

"How did it go, then?" I asked, in my most bored voice.

Though of course I was pretty curious. Posing around on a school stage somewhere, crooning about loving your "*momma*" and your "*familyyyy*";

I couldn't wait to hear how *that* had gone down.

"Yeah! Brilliant!!" said Sonny, obviously still buzzing on adrenaline as he bypassed me and headed into the living room, where he flopped down on one of the armchairs.

Wow; it was as if someone had shouted "Free money! Get your free money in the living room!", 'cause suddenly Will, Gran and Martha were rushing by me, settling themselves down, eyes glued to Sonny for his tales of showbiz wonderment.

"Well, darling?" said Nonna, on the edge of her (sofa) seat. "Was it fun?"

Everyone was waiting for Sonny's response, but Nonna's eyes were shining the fiercest. I thought about what Mum had told me about Nonna being a little bit disappointed all her life. Maybe she was now pinning all her hopes on Sonny, getting a huge buzz from his on-the-brink-of-possible-stardom ride.

I was a mature, sympathetic person (sometimes). I could understand that. Pity Nonna wasn't particularly mature or sympathetic enough to notice that while she focused a hundred and ten per cent on Sonny, she seemed oblivious to me. Except perhaps as a room-mate who got in the way of her shoe collection.

"It was great! Really amazing!"

"Was it exciting, being in front of a whole audience?" Letty asked breathlessly.

"Absolutely! We did four numbers for them, including the single, and then hung around doing autographs after!"

"Autographs!" gasped Gran, clasping a hand to her mouth, which made Martha blink her eyes with the surprise of it all. "How many did you have to do?"

"Oh . . . heaps!" Sonny shrugged, a well-chuffed smile slapped right across his face. "Think we've got a bit of a super-fan already!"

"Really? Who?" asked Nonna, a bit of a super-fan herself.

"A girl called Mel, who's, like, about fifteen or something. She asked us all to sign bits of paper '*To Mel, our number one fan, love, Sonny*', or whatever!"

Poor, deluded girl. She plainly needed serious psychiatric help.

"So you're getting proper fans already! Cool!" nodded Will. "So where next on your 'tour'?"

"We're doing a school in Mill Hill tomorrow!" Sonny answered, his smile so wide it was almost cracking his face.

Actually. . .

Wait a minute.

I sat back on the arm of the sofa and studied Sonny as he carried on with the question-and-answer session.

That smile – it didn't match the expression in his eyes. Something was going on.

For a minute or two, I couldn't figure it out, and then it dawned on me . . . Sonny was *acting*!!

"Oh, I should get you a drink, Sonny," said Gran, suddenly all a-twitter and getting to her feet, still cradling Martha.

"That's OK, I'm not thirsty," Sonny replied, getting to his feet himself. "I'm just going to go upstairs and have a shower."

"Oh, but you'll need one of your honey and lemons in hot water, for your voice, won't you?" Gran persisted.

Nonna looked like she was itching to make a comment about Gran fussing too much, but luckily Sonny spoke again, calling out to Gran as she headed towards the kitchen with Martha happily wedged on her hip.

"Um, OK – sure. Thanks, Gran," said Sonny, giving in. "I'll get it when I come down."

"And a sandwich?" Gran called after him.

"No, thanks!" yelled Sonny, stomping up the stairs.

With me right behind.

"Or a bit of quiche? Or a nice slice of cake?" Gran's voice drifted up.

"No, honestly – I'm not hungry!" shouted Sonny, not realizing at first that I was following him.

"Hey!"

I caught up with my brother on the landing. He turned his orange face to mine. It wasn't smiling any more.

"What's up?" he asked me as he kicked off his trainers and peeled off his T-shirt outside the bathroom door.

(I hoped he'd stop there. I didn't want to have to have this conversation with my hands covering my eyes.)

"Nothing's up with *me*," I said, trying not to pant. I still wanted to seem pretty uninterested, which is quite hard to do when you've rushed after someone taking two steps at a time up a staircase. "What's up with *you*?"

Sonny shifted his face into a what-are-you-talking-about? expression. But he wasn't fooling me.

"Sonny – if I had an Oscar on me I'd present it to you right now for that amazing bit of acting downstairs."

I swear I saw a hint of a telltale blush on his cheeks, but the orange foundation made it hard to say for sure.

 143

"What acting was I supposed to be doing?" he said defensively, yanking the socks off his feet.

(Not the shorts, *please*. I did not want a full-on view of his Superman pants, thank you very much.)

"When you pretended to Gran and Nonna and Will that everything went great at the showcase today," I challenged him.

"I wasn't acting! It went fine!"

"Liar."

Right now, if Mum was in, he'd be yelling, "Mum! Sadie says I'm a liar!", just to wind me up. Lucky for me she wasn't home yet, and he couldn't use that weapon against me.

"S'cuse me – I've got to have a shower," Sonny said, his face straight.

"So you're not going to tell me what really happened?" I egged him on, my arms crossed tightly in front of my chest.

"Nope," he said, going into the bathroom, his back to me.

Aha! I felt a little thrill – so something *must* have happened that he wasn't going to admit to!

Then I felt something else . . . warm, moist socks hitting me on the face, just a millisecond before the bathroom door shut and locked.

Yuck. . .

Friend of a freak

It was Wednesday, it was four o'clock, and I was about to be lightly humiliated.

Me and Letitia had come to the branch of Waterstone's down at the Angel, Islington after school. I was thinking about buying a thesaurus (my English teacher told our class today that owning one would help us improve our vocabulary) and Letty was going to buy a nice postcard if they had any.

Whatever, here we were.

And there was the youngish guy behind the till, looking at the book I was buying.

Then he looked at me.

Then he looked back at the book I was buying.

Then he looked at me again, like I was a freak.

"It's not for me, it's for a friend," I said, all spikily, as I felt my cheeks flush pink.

How dumb of me. I shouldn't have cared *what*

 145

he thought, *or* bothered trying to explain myself to him.

OK, so now he didn't think *I* was a freak, but that I had a *friend* who was a freak, which made me a friend of a freak, which in itself was a bit freaky, I guess.

"Uh, that'll be £6.99," he mumbled, sliding *London's Cemeteries* across the counter at me as if I'd just bought something creepy and weird, like a book about how to torture ladybirds for fun or something.

I mean, what was the point in a bookshop selling guide books to the cemeteries of London if the staff gave funny looks to every thirteen-year-old girl who came in to buy one?

OK, I don't suppose it happened too often. . .

"He'll probably really like that," said Letitia as we walked away from the counter, out through the wide doors and into the sunshine.

"Yeah, hopefully," I answered her, thinking that I was . . .

a) glad that I got bored shopping for a thesaurus and stumbled upon this book instead – I hoped it might cheer Cormac up after the disappointment of his old friends being useless at the weekend

b) confused that Letty seemed ever-so-slightly annoyed with me. She hadn't been when we wandered down here after school and first came in. What was all *that* about? It was the same sort of huffiness she came out with if I let slip I'd been shopping with Hannah and without *her.*

"Of course, Cormac might have it already!" Letty suddenly suggested, sounding now as if she was slightly pleased at the idea, even though if it was true, it would spoil my nice gesture.

I didn't get it. And I didn't have the energy to get it. Nonna wasn't just snoring now; she'd started talking in her sleep last night. Well, not so much talking in her sleep as shouting in Spanish at her builder. I tried whispering "Nonna!" at her to shake her out of her dream/nightmare, moved on to giving her a gentle shake, and then when *that* didn't work, I took the foam off four of her rollers and pinged them in the direction of her head (couldn't actually see where I was aiming in the pitch-black). It didn't make any difference, of course, but it made me feel a bit better.

I spent the rest of the night half-awake, half-asleep with my useless earplugs in and a pillow wedged over my head. I was tired. I didn't have enough functioning brain cells left to figure out what was wrong with Letty.

I only had enough to remember where the stop was where I could hop on a bus up to Dad's place. I usually had my tea with him on Wednesdays (Sonny too, if he wasn't rehearsing), but today it was just going to be a quick hello/goodbye, because we'd be having a farewell tea for Nonna tonight to celebrate (no, not the appropriate word), er, wish her bon voyage for her flight back home to Spain tomorrow.

"That's my bus. Better run!" I told Letty, spotting the No. 19.

"Hmm," muttered Letty, confusingly. . .

"Letty thought you might have this already," I told Cormac ten minutes later, when I came across him in Dad's flat, being made to eat a pre-tea omelette by Gran.

Cormac blushed the deepest cherry red known to man.

Uh-oh.

"It's no big deal!" I quickly assured him, panicking in case he read too much into the present. "I just thought it was the sort of thing you'd think was interesting!"

Urgh, I was starting to blush myself. Why had this suddenly turned weird?

"Yeah, I get that. Sorry. No, it's great," waffled Cormac, the cherry red starting to fade.

Too complicated, don't understand . . . my over-tired brain complained.

Cormac glanced around. We seemed to be alone – Gran was loudly humming some show tune in the kitchen while she happily washed dusters, while Dad was in the loo with the radio blaring "Teenage Kicks" by the Undertones (in his Top Ten of favourite-ever tracks).

"It's just when you mentioned Letty," said Cormac.

"It's just when I mentioned Letty *what*?" I practically repeated back to him, trying to get a handle on what he was saying.

"It just made me remember something my mates said on Sunday," Cormac carried on, starting to blush cherry red all over again. I wished he wouldn't. It clashed really badly with his hair.

"Which was?" I tried to prompt him.

"They said she . . . well . . . that it was obvious that she fancied me. From the way she was looking over."

Uh-oh. Letty's manic crushes were mighty and strong, but they vanished just as quickly as they came (till she had a mighty and strong crush on someone else). The good thing was that none of her crushees up till now had the *faintest* idea that they were her current Fantasy Boyfriend, and that was exactly how it had to stay.

Specially in Cormac's case, for two reasons: 1) he was my mate and so was she, and I didn't want any awkwardness if they met up, and 2) he was four years older than us, which made him creepily elderly for genuine boyfriend material.

"That is absolute rubbish!" I lied, saving Letty's pride, and in the same moment realizing that she'd been snippy with me earlier because she was a little bit jealous of the idea of me giving her Fantasy Boyfriend a present. Sigh. . .

"Really?" sighed Cormac, looking well relieved.

"No *way* does she fancy you!" I lied again, sounding very indignant on the part of my secretly lovestruck friend. "They were just trying to wind you up!"

"Yeah? Yeah, they *were*, weren't they?" said Cormac, relaxing and slowly returning to his usual milk-white colouring.

"Absolutely!" I said with a definite nod, thinking I was such a good actress that I should audition for that stupid stage school that Sonny went to.

Buzzzzzzzzzzzzzzz, went the intercom.

Speak of the devil. It had to be Sonny, who said he'd drop by here too, once he got back from today's showcase at a school in Enfield.

Wonder if it went as well as the one in Mill Hill yesterday and the one the day before that? I thought wryly to myself as I bounded over and picked up the intercom phone on the wall to buzz him in. He'd been lying again yesterday too, of course. Through his teeth. I'd stared intently at him while he'd twittered about how fantastic the gig had gone, hoping I'd instantly develop the psychic connection twins are meant to have and be able to see the truth sloshing about in his pea-sized brain.

"Hello?" I said, putting on a sort of stupid, squeaky girly voice. (*Told* you I should audition for Sonny's stage school.)

"Who's that?" asked Sonny, sounding fuzzy on the other end of the intercom, down by the front door, next to the undertakers' shop.

"Oh, Sonny. . ." I said in the stupid, squeaky, girly voice. "It's Mel; I've missed you *so* much. . ."

"Oh, shut up, Sadie, and let me in!" he ordered, sounding like he was half-laughing, half-annoyed.

"She didn't turn up again today, did she?" I asked, standing by the open door to the flat as Sonny bounded up the stairs, in Lycra and orange foundation.

"Yes, she did," he said, coming breathlessly in to the hall and hanging his stuff up in a pile on the floor.

"Who's this?" asked Cormac, his ears pricking up.

"Sonny's band – they have a super-fan!" said Gran, coming out of the kitchen, shaking a wrung-out duster in her hands. "Is that right? Is that what you call it, Sonny?"

"No – you call it a *stalker*," I jumped in, arching my (one good) eyebrow at my brother as I led the way back into Dad's living room.

"She's not a *stalker*, Sadie. She's just really into the band!" said Sonny, looking like he was trying to convince himself.

"Yeah, and since she met you on Monday, she's bunked off her school early *two* days in a row to follow you to your other North London gigs. That's *creepy*!"

"Oh, no, I'm sure she's just enthusiastic, Sadie," suggested Gran.

"Enthusiastically *creepy*," I muttered under my breath.

Sonny ignored me, and seemed intent on speaking to Cormac.

"Hey, we did a workshop this morning at school, yeah?"

"Er, yeah?" replied Cormac, who probably could've said "Hey, I did a burial today, yeah?" in return.

"And it was this guy called Martin Shore, and he's an ex-student of my school, and he's a comedian who's just got his first nationwide tour!"

It was like someone had turned up the brightness dial on Cormac. He sat up, instantly alert.

"Martin Shore? I haven't heard of him. But wow, that must be brilliant for him. . ."

"He's dead excited. The tour's happening in a few weeks' time, and he's doing tons of small warm-up gigs and stuff before it. I spoke to him after the workshop and I told him about you –"

Cormac might as well have been hit by lightning. He was rigid with shock. The plate with the omelette slid off his lap, along with *London's Cemeteries*. He lunged to grab the plate, the egg and the book, but Gran got there first, ever helpful.

"– and he said he'd arrange to get us a couple of tickets for a show sometime soon, and you can go backstage and meet him!"

It was a really cool (sorry to steal your word, Will) present that Sonny had given Cormac there. *Much* better than the stupid guide book of cemeteries that Gran was currently wiping greasy egg off (with a confused expression as she read the title and looked at the stone angel on the cover).

"Sonny! Didn't hear you come in!" Dad boomed as he wandered back in the room.

"Maybe because you had 6 Music blaring in the loo," I pointed out.

"Well, there's no such thing as having good music too loud!" Dad joked.

I was about to say that the neighbours might disagree when I remembered that Dad's immediate neighbours were either a) Cormac, or b) dead.

Anyway, I knew that Dad was probably on the verge of asking Sonny how the showcases went, but before my brother got into some long-winded ramble about how they'd (supposedly) gone, I needed to remind him of something important.

"Listen – I know you just got here, Sonny, but we're supposed to be home early-ish tonight, remember, because it's Nonna's going-away tea."

"But didn't you get Mum's text?" said Sonny and Dad, in spooky unison. They were sometimes (dopily) more similar than me and Sonny, even though *we* were the twins.

"No," I mumbled, rifling in my bag for the mobile that I must have – oops – forgotten to switch back on once I got out of school.

"Well, it turns out—"

That was Dad, starting to explain Mum's message.

At the same time, my thumb was already pressing buttons madly, trying to locate Mum's text to me.

But before Dad could speak or Mum's message could ping on screen, I figured out what the Nonna news was.

"She's not going back tomorrow, is she?" I said, picturing my old room, still damp and dusty with plaster, with plasterers not booked to come till a week on Tuesday.

Then I pictured my current room, which had become more and more Nonna's boudoir over the days, with me as an unwelcome squatter on my easily-deflatable, farty-sounding blow-up bed.

"Nope. The builders are behind schedule on her flat," said Dad. "She'll be here for at least another week."

I felt myself deflate as quickly as a punctured airbed. . .

A surprise someone to the rescue

"Are you busy with your homework, Sadie, sweetheart?" asked Nonna, putting her head around the bedroom door.

"Yes," I lied, sitting up straight and studiously in front of my computer.

Actually, it was a *half*-lie, 'cause I genuinely *should've* been researching a thing on the Industrial Revolution (spinning jennies, to be precise, whatever *they* were).

Instead, I'd been gossiping via email to Hannah, telling her about Spanish builders and their over-running schedule, about Nonna sleep-shouting and about the Sadie Rocks mini-tour and Mel the Stalker.

In return, Hannah had told me about Harry putting poster paint in the shower gel and her dad turning blue. She was also wondering if Sonny knew if his band's mini-tour was coming to *her* school. When Nonna walked in, I was just in the middle of asking Hannah whether she was more interested in the possibility of checking out the band or the stalker.

"Now *where's* my address book gone. . ." said Nonna, rifling around on the surface of the dressing table, amongst all her lotions and potions.

"Think it's on my bedside table," I said helpfully, though the bedside table wasn't really "mine" at the moment.

"Thank you, dear. I'll have to phone my friend Angela and tell her that I won't be back in time for her and her husband's golden-anniversary party this weekend. Oh, those builders! I'm so cross I honestly feel like swearing. But I'd have to do it in Spanish so as not to offend your young ears!"

Funny. That was pretty funny, Nonna. I gave her a wry smile and she shot me one right back.

"You know, you look very pretty when you smile, Sadie, even if it is a bit lopsided," said Nonna, being kind and tactless all in one go. Sigh. . .

"It gives me character," I said, repeating what Mum once told me when I moaned to her about my crooked smile.

"Of course, you're right, darling," Nonna replied,

backing down as she flicked through her notebook. "By the way, I was just saying to your mum that you and Sonny are surely just about old enough to fly out to Spain without her. If either of you ever wanted to come for a visit during the holidays – together or even on your own – just let me know. I'll pay for the flights, and we'd have a lovely time!"

"Uh, thank you," I told Generous Nonna.

The idea of hopping on a plane on my own – waved off by Mum or Dad at one end and picked up at the other by Nonna – was deliciously exciting. But the reality of hanging out with Nonna on my own was kind of scary. With no one else around, I'd have an undiluted Nonna all to myself, and I didn't think I could handle it.

And the idea of the alternative – being stuck in a small-ish flat with both Nonna and Sonny . . . well, that would be more like torture than a treat.

"You know, I *really* don't know what's wrong with books!" Nonna suddenly announced out of nowhere, her eyes and fingers still searching for the elusive phone number.

"Huh?" I turned my head around from the computer and gazed at her in confusion.

"It's *pardon*, Sadie, dear, or *excuse me*, not *huh*!"

She laughed, but it was annoying anyway. "I mean that I don't understand why you youngsters don't just go to the library and borrow books for your homework instead of using the silly internet!"

"Nonna, I *do* still use books for my assignments, but the internet is great when you need something right away and aren't near a library," I tried to explain, wondering if, from that angle, she could see I was on my email application and not some worthy educational site.

Nope – think I was safe.

"But the internet is full of rubbish like gossip and chat rooms with *stalkers* and all sorts in them!"

Ha – I was hardly likely to get myself a stalker by researching spinning jennies, or even checking out some of my favourite sites, like the one with photos of cats curled up in sinks (too cute. . .). *Sonny* was the one with the stalker – a real live one.

"Nonna, I don't go to any chat rooms," I tried to reassure her. "I only use the internet for homework or to look up fun stuff."

"What sort of 'fun' stuff?" Nonna asked, looking up at me sharply.

"Teenage sites – stuff about music and films and whatever. I don't know!" I said vaguely, sensing that Nonna was suddenly in the mood for a rant.

I toyed with quickly calling up the cats-in-sinks site to show her. But then I didn't know whether she'd think it was adorable or ridiculous, or turn into Mad Nonna and claim the kitten snoozing in the old-fashioned butler sink was very possibly a forty-seven-year-old dodgy male stalker in disguise.

"But teenagers nowadays spend too much time sitting in their rooms on computers when they *should* be outside in the fresh air!"

"I *do* get fresh air, Nonna," I answered wearily. "I go to the park with my friends."

"Ah, now *parks*!" said Nonna, waving a finger around in the air. "You can get some very *strange* people hanging around in parks! I mean, I read in the paper only yesterday that—"

Ping!

Incoming email. I clicked it open, glad of something to distract me from Nonna's rambling.

Is she doing your head in? I could hear her when I passed your door just now. Say if you need help! S

Wow. Sonny. I'd normally rather eat a bowl of Clyde's rabbit food than accept help from my brother. But these were desperate times. . .

HELP!!! I typed back, my return email instantly pinging thousands of miles into space to some satellite, and then pinging right back down to

Sonny's computer in his room at the end of the hall.

"—and those are the honest statistics; it said so in the *Daily Mail*, so it just goes to show—"

I didn't know what the statistics were or what they went to show, but Nonna didn't seem to notice that I hadn't been hanging on her every word. I found myself wondering if there were times when she didn't really want a conversation – maybe she was just happy having an audience for her monologues.

KNOCK, KNOCK, KNOCK.

"Come in!" Nonna called out before I could, showing whose room she considered this to be. "Oh, hello, Sonny, darling! What can I do for you?"

"Um, I need Sadie, actually. Sadie – I'm really, really stuck on my maths homework. Can you come and give me a hand?"

Sonny looked confused and troubled, as though a whole bunch of equations were giving him a really hard time. He was a good actor, I had to admit. If I hadn't just put an SOS out to him just now, I'd have been convinced that maths genuinely was melting his brain.

"Sure!!" I said enthusiastically, leaping to my feet as if helping Sonny with his homework was the biggest thrill of the day. (I couldn't remember the last time I genuinely *had* helped him – maybe when we were eight? When we were doing the project on the Great Fire of London and he'd fallen behind with class stuff 'cause at night he was starring in this North London drama production of *Oliver*?)

"Thanks!" I said, gratefully slamming the door to Sonny's room shut. I walked over to the window and threw it open, gazing at the view of the garden, and of the copse where our pet Christmas tree hung out, and at the glimpses of ancient granite and marble headstones in the graveyard beyond.

Ooh, that looked peaceful.

Maybe I could get our tent out of the shed and camp there . . . right in the middle of the trees, I mused to myself, till I realized there would be too many mysterious things that went *clunk*, *tweet* and *rustle* in the night. I wouldn't sleep a wink.

"No worries," said Sonny, flopping down on to a chair by his desk.

I turned round to look at him – and to gaze at what used to be Dad's bachelor pad, where the three of us often hung out, listening to music and talking rubbish – and saw something that surprised me.

"You really *are* doing maths homework!" I said, pointing at the book by his hand.

"*Duh!* What kind of homework did you expect me to do?" Sonny grinned.

"Well . . . maybe a project on great mime artists of the world; or an essay on why tap-dancing's not silly, even if it looks it; or figuring out stage directions for a play about space-fish. *I* dunno, whatever it is that you do at stage school!"

"*Theatre* school," Sonny corrected me (as usual). "Anyway, yes, we get homework for our theatre-studies subjects, but we still have to do all the regular subjects as well, same as you!"

Oh. I hadn't thought about that. How did he manage to cram all that stuff into one day at school, plus have a whole ton of homework and band rehearsals on top?

It made me come over all exhausted (though maybe that was down to disrupted sleep).

I slid down the wall and ended up cross-legged on the floor.

"So the show went well today?" I asked my brother, knowing that the answer would be yes – at least that's what he told Mum, Dad, Gran and Nonna earlier, when he came in all smiles.

"It was OK," he answered, shrugging.

Oooh, there was definitely something he wasn't

telling me. But I didn't feel like wheedling it out of him right now; not when he'd been almost human and helped me escape from Nonna.

"So . . . was your stalker there?" I asked.

"Yep – and get this!" said Sonny, suddenly more animated. "I just heard from Alan—"

"That's 'Hal', right?" I said, checking I'd got the stage-name right.

"Yeah, that's him. Anyway, he walked home from the gig 'cause it was in Palmers Green and he lives round the corner, right?"

"Right."

"Anyway, that girl Mel *followed* him! He said she stood outside his front garden for an hour, till she finally got bored and went home!"

"Yew! Creepy!" I muttered.

"Totally!" Sonny nodded. "But I just spoke to Benny, and Alan told him about what happened, so maybe he'll talk to someone at her school or something. Anyway, get this –"

Great, more gossip. This was much better than being lectured and confused by Nonna.

"– Benny's been contacted by the *Highbury and Islington Gazette*, and they want to do a piece on me! Y'know – local boy makes good, that kind of thing!"

"What – just *you*? Not the whole band?" I checked, wondering if his ego was so enormous that he'd blocked out Kennedy, Marcus, Hal and Ziggy at the first mention of publicity.

"Nope – it's just me. The others don't live in Highbury or Islington, so that's why they just want to interview *me*."

"Wow. So . . . are you looking forward to it?" I asked, trying to sound interested but in a very offhand way.

"Kind of. But they want to do it this Saturday, and they've asked to come here and interview me in my room."

Sonny was frowning, looking round the large, above-the-garage room that had once doubled (trebled?) as Dad's bedroom, living room and home office. Mum had suggested Sonny move in here instead of me, since it was big enough for him to practise his dance steps in. (And only the car in the garage downstairs would be disturbed by all the thumping.)

"So, what's wrong with that?" I asked, seeing from Sonny's face that he definitely thought something was. Wrong with it, I mean.

"Well, it's not very rock 'n' roll, is it, for someone who's in a band?"

His *band* wasn't exactly rock 'n' roll, but I didn't say that aloud, since I wasn't Nonna at her tactless best.

"It's OK," I said, glancing around at the white walls, adorned with just a couple of lonely posters for Arsenal Football Club and *Joseph And The Amazing Technicolor Dreamcoat* (yep, Sonny wanted to get into the rainbow jacket one day). "I mean, you've got your guitar there *and* your CD collection."

"Yeah, but it's not got much else going for it. I've been too busy with the band to fix it up. . ."

Though he'd found time to drop quite a lot of clothes on the floor and shove a couple of dirty plates under the bed, I noticed.

"Hey, I was thinking, do you fancy –"

Straightaway, I knew what Sonny was going to say: did I fancy helping him style the place, so it looked like some cool rock star hang-out by Saturday.

But actually, I'd just had an amazing idea. One that involved Cormac. I was just about to tell Sonny what it was when I suddenly tuned into the rest of his sentence.

"– moving in here with me for a bit, since Nonna's driving you crazy? I'd tidy up and everything, and you could have the bed. I don't mind taking a turn on the blow-up mattress."

The very idea had made me feel ill when I'd half-heartedly thought about it before. But now . . .

oh, the sheer luxury of a *real* bed! And no snoring or shouting in Spanish!

I could do it.

I'd have to fumigate all the sheets first, of course, and I'd have to put up with Sonny's incessant chatting. Still, that wasn't too much of a problem; it was rude to tell your grandmother to shut up, but perfectly acceptable to do it to your brother.

"You're on!" I said, so thrilled I could've hugged him, only *that*, of course, would be *way* too icky. . .

You are being watched. . .

Coming home from school on Friday, I saw Will in front of me, pushing Martha's buggy with one hand and a strange black metal contraption on wheels with the other.

It wasn't going very well. Think of someone trying to manoeuvre two shopping trolleys at the same time and you get the idea.

"What's this?" I'd asked him, hurrying to catch up with my my not-quite-stepdad and baby sister.

"An old clothes rail," he'd explained, nodding at the PLEASE HELP YOURSELF note taped on to it. "It was on the pavement outside someone's house down the road."

"Do we need a clothes rail?" I'd asked, thinking of the cavernous antique pine wardrobe in Mum and Will's room and the plain IKEA wardrobes in me and Sonny's rooms.

"*You* do!" Will had said with a grin, and wouldn't tell me any more.

But it started to become clear once we got home.

"Ta-na!" Will said, after a rummage in the airing cupboard. He was holding up the spare pair of curtains that used to be in my old room.

"Ta-na!" translated as privacy.

With a quick unscrew of one end of the clothes rail, which was by now in Sonny's room, Will slid on the old curtains and instantly created a screen.

Ta-na! Me and Sonny both had our own chunk of room. (OK, so it reminded me a bit of the curtains round hospital beds, but I appreciated the thought.)

By the way, Nonna wasn't around to help out/admire/criticize Will's efforts – she was using her unexpectedly extended holiday to go visit an exhibition at the Transport Museum in Covent Garden. Though knowing her, she'd probably end up at the Transport Museum in Coventry.

Oh, and *another* by the way, she hadn't taken it personally on Thursday when I relocated to Sonny's room. I spoke to Mum first, and we came up with this big waffle about how we wanted Nonna to feel as comfortable and welcome as possible during her extended stay, blah, blah, blah, but we needn't have gone to the trouble. Before

Mum had finished saying her spiel, Nonna was already excitedly planning to rearrange my/her room, shifting table lamps and rows of shoes while Will was still in the middle of humphing out my blow-up bed.

So Sonny's room was my home-from-home (well, room-from-room) for the meantime. But it wasn't where I was right now.

Nope.

I was in a flat that should feature in an interiors magazine. Maybe one called *Bizarre Homes & Gardens*.

"Move anything you like anywhere you want," Cormac's twenty-four-year-old brother, Kyle, was nonchalantly telling the bemused photographer from the local paper. "I totally understand that you might want to style the shot."

Kyle was just back from his fashion shoot in sunny faraway somewhere, with a light tan showing on his skinny arms and face, and sun-kissed highlights on his expensively messy hair and tiny goatee.

Letty – perched on the edge of the sofa, as if she shouldn't be here – gazed at Kyle in awe, as if he was a celebrity or something. Hannah – curling herself up comfortably on the retro, egg-yolk-yellow swivelling chair – acted all casual, as if she hung out here all the time. (Ha – she'd only been here once before, and her chin had practically bungee-jumped to the floor and back in shock when she saw how crazy and amazing the place was.)

"Cormac – I'll leave you to be host; I've got to unpack this lot. . ." Kyle said over his shoulder, as he dragged two heavy suitcases (one for clothes, one for his work-related make-up and hair stuff) through to his bedroom.

I'd never seen inside Kyle's room, or Cormac's, for that matter. The living room made me giddy enough.

"Interesting place!" said the young girl reporter, gawping around at the red walls, the black chandelier, the gold-sprayed granddad clock, the huge seventies sofa, the giant silver and black prints of famous people on the wall, and the knitted suit of armour hanging on a mannequin in the corner. (Who could forget *that* in a hurry?)

"My brother collects things from photo shoots he goes on. And he likes collecting stuff from flea markets," Cormac explained to the girl reporter.

"And you are?" she asked, with a notebook, as well as a tape machine, in her hand.

She was looking Cormac up and down, trying to make sense of this guy in a sober black suit and tie standing in the middle of this kitsch-fest.

"Cormac McConnell. I'm a friend of Sonny's."

"*And* he's a comedian!" Sonny leapt in, keen to give Cormac a bit of free publicity while he had the chance.

"Ok*aaaay*. . ." said the girl dubiously, not really convinced, I could tell. "And *you're* Sonny's sister. *Obviously*."

Her pen was pointing at me.

"Never seen him before in my life," I joked feebly. I never particularly liked being compared physically to Sonny. It was like being told I looked like a *boy*.

"She's Sadie. The band's named after her!" Sonny jumped in, though the interview proper hadn't started yet – the photographer had to do his bit first, because he needed to get away and snap the mayor officially opening a new disabled ramp somewhere (oh, the glamour).

"Really? So you're the *real* Sadie!" said the reporter. "That must make you feel very proud!"

"Not exactly," I squirmed. Specially since the phrase "Sadie rocks!" started out as a sarcastic comment one of Sonny's mates once made. . .

I really wished the reporter girl wouldn't talk to me. I'd fixed it with Cormac so that Sonny could do his piece with the local paper here; that was my good deed – in exchange for Sonny letting me doss down in his room – and that was as far as it went.

I'd have made my excuses and left them to it right then and there, but both Hannah and Letty had been pretty keen to come along and listen in on Sonny's first-ever interview. Well, *Letty* had seemed pretty keen, while Hannah had been all yeah-whatever about it, but I was pretty sure it would have taken a herd of wildebeest to keep her away today.

"Sorry – can I move you?" we all heard the photographer say to Hannah. "Think I'd like to get Sonny sitting there. . ."

Hannah unfurled her legs and jumped out of the chair as if it was electrified the minute the photographer spoke to her. (Was that a giggle from Letty? You bet.)

"Fans?" I heard the reporter ask Sonny. I turned to see her nodding first at the smirking Letty, and then at the trying-to-regain-her-cool Hannah.

"Uh, well, no. Just friends," said Sonny, looking in the giant wall mirror and running a hand across his head, trying to spike up his already-spiked hair.

"Oh. But the girl downstairs definitely is!"

"*What* girl?" asked Sonny, whipping his head around at the reporter's words.

"The one standing outside the funeral director's. She's got an autograph book. About fifteen-ish. . .?"

It was a race to the window, but Sonny, me, Hannah and Letty let Cormac do the opening, in case we pulled up the sash and made it squeak noisily.

We didn't want the fan to look up and catch us staring down at her.

"*Is* it her?" I asked in a whisper, gazing down at the top of a dark head of hair.

At that second, some sixth sense must have told Mel the mega-fan that five people were gawping at her from a second-storey window. She lifted her chin and gawped back up at us.

"It's *her*!!" gasped Sonny, leaping back from the window as if he'd just spotted a tidal wave coming, or a large swarm of killer bees.

The leaping was catching – me, Hannah and Cormac did it too.

"How did she know where you'd be?" asked Letty, still hanging out of the window and frowning down at the girl.

"I've read about stalkers in celebrity magazines," said Hannah. "They have almost criminal minds. They go through your bins and find out all sorts of stuff about you!"

I wouldn't go through our bins back at home, if

I was Mel the mega-fan. All she'd find was a bunch of regular rubbish with the added urgh factor of cat litter and rabbit poo. Don't think she'd learn much about Sonny from *that*.

In the background, I could hear the faint *scritch-scratch* of the reporter's pen. I figured Sonny's stalker would be getting a mention in his piece in the paper.

"D'you think she'll still be there when I go down?" asked Sonny, looking worried.

Good grief, his band hadn't even had a record out and he was already getting spooked by mad fans.

"Don't worry – we'll smuggle you out," I told him.

"How?" Sonny frowned.

I nodded my head towards the knitted suit of armour.

"No way!" exclaimed Sonny.

"Well, it's either that, or in a coffin. Right, Cormac?"

"Right!" nodded Cormac, joining in with my mickey-taking.

"Shut up, Sadie!" said Sonny, sussing he was being mercilessly teased.

"Shut up yourself, Sonny!" I said back, giving him my best *I-got-you!* lopsided grin.

Scritch-scratch-scritch went the reporter's pen.

"Can we have you on the chair now, Sonny?" asked the photographer.

As he went, Sonny shot me a look that made me think I might have his sweaty socks lobbed at me again soon – this time over the clothes-rail curtain when I was trying to get to sleep – but it sure was worth it for the sheer pleasure of winding him up. . .

Our (deathly) day out

Coffins and knitted suits of armour were not required.

After the interview, me, Sonny, Hannah and Letty hid out downstairs in Dad's flat. We watched old episodes of *Futurama* with Dad till Cormac phoned up from the shop below (can you call an undertaker's a *shop*?) and told us that Mel the mega-fan had given up and gone home.

Phew.

Hurray for Cormac, counter-spying on Sonny's spying stalker.

And hurray that Cormac really, *really* liked the I'm-sorry-your-friends-are-rubbish present that I'd given him. I hadn't been sure that he was all that thrilled with *London's Cemeteries* the other day, but then I guess I couldn't blame him for being dazzled and sidetracked by Sonny's promise to introduce him to a real, live, professional comedian sometime.

Whatever, me and Cormac spent nearly the whole of Sonny's interview in the kitchen, leafing through *London's Cemeteries* and planning a day out. A deathly day out. And get this: it turned out Cormac had already read bits of the book to Dad that morning (over scrambled eggs on toast, courtesy of Gran), and Dad had said, "Pick a graveyard, any graveyard, and I'll drive you guys there tomorrow!"

So, for our deathly day out, me and Cormac toyed firstly with going to St Paul's Church, across the piazza from the Transport Museum in Covent Garden: that's where there're memorials to people like silent movie star Charlie Chaplin, and the grave of a heart-throb highwayman called Claude Duval.

Then we thought about spooky Highgate Cemetery, where writer Bram Stoker got the inspiration for the story of *Dracula*. (Brrr. . .)

We'd ended up settling on Hammersmith Old Burial Ground, 'cause of a gravestone there that was apparently carved in the shape of a bed and pillow, and was the last resting place of the excellently named Sexton Cisbert van Os (and his wife, Ms Os).

But hey, Sunday had come, and we weren't anywhere near Covent Garden, Highgate or

Hammersmith; we were in my garden. Well, *practically*.

At least, we were in the graveyard that backed on to our house, drifting around, having a competition to find the quirkiest name on a gravestone, though we knew we'd never find anything to beat old Sexton Cisbert van Os. (Not forgetting Mrs Os, of course.)

"*Evangeline Ethel Cramp?*" suggested Sonny.

Yep, instead of Dad, me and Cormac had my brother for company. Yesterday afternoon, after our *Futurama* session, Dad had a big order come in out of the blue, and sadly had to spend Sunday up to his neck in disposable tableware instead of schlepping round graveyards with me and Cormac.

And Sonny? Well, when I asked him if he wanted to tag along this afternoon, he'd stopped practising star jumps for the finale of the schools' showcase and came like a shot. (Maybe star jumps and harmonizing "*Love is lovely, love is lovely!!*" was getting to be too much like hard work?)

"Yeah, that's pretty good," I admitted, while peeling back the ivy covering the lettering on a nearby stone. "*Cyril Iolanthe Ponsonby. . .*" I read aloud.

What strangely old-fashioned names. Even with

the current craze for great-granny and great-granddaddy names, I didn't suppose there'd be many Evangeline Ethels and Cyril Iolanthes in nurseries anytime soon.

Cormac wasn't joining in; he was leaning against a giant stone angel, thumbing through the book again.

"It's not in there, is it?" I asked, stumbling over some overgrown bramble bushes towards him. "This cemetery, I mean?"

"Nah, not big or important enough. But thanks again for this, Sadie – it's really . . . y'know. Interesting."

Hmm. He didn't *look* a hundred per cent interested. He looked sort of *frowny*. (What a useless description: I should have bought that thesaurus from the bookshop after all.)

"You all right, Cormac?" asked Sonny, wading through the undergrowth to join us.

"Yeah . . . no . . . I mean, yeah, but I was just thinking about my mates and last Sunday. And thinking I haven't heard from any of them since then."

Oh . . . it wasn't a great feeling, having your friends go flaky on you. I guess I was lucky; Letty and Hannah were always pretty cool. All I had to worry about with them was slight jealous huffs

(Letty, over Cormac) and contamination with horrible brothers (Hannah, and Harry the Weasel).

I tried to think of something helpful to say.

"Well, you know, sometimes friendships sort of, um, wither by the wayside. . ."

Wow, that was lame. I couldn't believe I was quoting Nonna. The trouble is, I'm great at sarcasm, but kind of lousy at comforting.

"Yeah. Well, I was thinking that I'm OK with it. If I don't really hang out with those guys any more, I mean."

Good. I was glad Cormac thought about it that way.

And I was glad Cormac didn't mind being friends with thirteen-year-olds like us and forty-something-year-olds like my dad.

You just like who you like, don't you? Not who you're supposed to. Same went for love; Gran loved Martha and Martha loved Gran, even though they weren't related. And I was related to Nonna, who I'd first met when I was just a few hours old, but felt closer to Will, who I'd only known for the last couple of years.

"Yeah, well, if they're not into what you're doing, Cormac, then they're losers," said Sonny, making a comment that sounded a lot better than my "withering by the wayside" waffle. Still, it was pretty ironic for Sonny to come out with that, when he had a big-headed, small-brained, wide-faced loser of a best friend himself.

Sonny's phone suddenly burbled into life (was it Kennedy, the loser?). The electronic jingle sounded weird in a Victorian graveyard filled with wildflowers and butterflies.

"Hey!" Sonny said, into the receiver. "No! . . . Yeah? . . . *Really?!*"

There was quite a few more *no!, yeah?, really?!*s before me and Cormac caught on to what the other half of the conversation was about.

Ziggy (i.e., Gordon) was telling Sonny that Marcus (i.e., Mark) had opened his bedroom curtains this morning – dressed only in Scooby Doo boxers – to see Mel the Stalker watching him. He didn't manage to close the curtains before she held out her phone and snapped a photo. When his parents had gone outside a couple of minutes later, she'd vanished. (Bet she'd run home to download her prized photo. She might have it blown up life-size and stuck on her wall by now, for all we knew.)

Then an hour later, Ziggy had seen a girl that looked a *lot* like Mel in his street when he was cycling to the newsagent's to get the Sunday papers for his parents.

"Where do you think she is now?" Sonny wondered aloud at the end of the phone call, gazing worriedly around the cemetery, as if Mel might be hiding behind the grave of Cyril Iolanthe Ponsonby with her zoom lens.

"Outside Kennedy's house, probably! He's the only one not to have been stalked yet, isn't he?"

As the jokey words left my mouth, I stopped dead.

"What?" asked Cormac, seeing me freeze.

Yeah, what? What had I just seen? A drift of white dress, wafting between distant gravestones.

Mel the mega-fan pinged into my mind straightaway, but that drift of a white dress didn't really fit with the girl I'd caught a glimpse of yesterday – all dark hair, primary-coloured T-shirt and cropped jeans.

Or maybe it was the ghost of Evangeline Ethel Cramp, come to spook us for sniggering at her name.

Most likely, it was just a plastic carrier bag fluttering in the wind.

So what I'd seen was either a stalker, a ghost or a plastic bag.

"Well?" said Cormac, still waiting, all concerned, for an answer.

"Ouch, I've got stung by a nettle!" I lied, coming to life and rubbing my leg.

Didn't want to share my thoughts of ghostly plastic bags or whatever and have Sonny tease me stupid. That would be *no* fun. Not like when I was teasing *him*.

"D'you want to look for more dumb names?" Sonny asked me.

"Nah," I said, feigning a limp. "Let's go home. Let's have a cup of tea with Nonna and have a competition to see which one of us she winds up first!"

Sonny and Cormac both laughed. Good. I'd managed to cover up the fact that I'd got a tiny bit spooked just there. . .

18

Unleash the secret weapon. . .

I won.

It was me.

Nonna got to me first.

"I'm just not sure it's appropriate, Sadie. Not at *your* age."

Nonna was sitting in the kitchen, striking an elegant pose on the chair in her red and orange kaftan as she sipped her jasmine tea (made by me).

I wanted to scream. But I couldn't – Cormac was upstairs in Sonny's room, and I didn't want him to hear what Nonna was wittering on about, or I'd never be able to look him in the eye again, same as Letty never would if he ever found out he was (cringe) her Fantasy Boyfriend.

Anyway, what was the problem? Well, Nonna had convinced herself that Cormac was my *real* boyfriend.

How wildly, stupidly annoying and just plain *wrong* was that?!

"Well, all I'm saying is, I just don't know if *I'd* have been very keen on it. Not if *I* were your mum."

Arrghhh! The urge to scream was still strong, but Kennedy had arrived and was up in Sonny's room too, and I didn't fancy *him* catching on and spending the next seventeen years teasing me stupid, thank you very much.

Then, bingo! I remembered the secret weapon I was saving to use in an emergency.

"Well, you're *not* my mum – you're my *granny*!" I pointed out, enjoying seeing her wince under the word.

Granny! Granny! Granny! I felt like shouting some more, but stopped myself – I didn't want to seem as juvenile as Nonna was treating me.

"*What* wouldn't you be keen on, if you were me?" Mum asked Nonna, appearing in the doorway all freshly showered and with her hair wrapped in a towel.

"Sadie going on a *date* with a *seventeen-year-old* boy to a *graveyard*," said Nonna, making it sound like I'd gone on a *joyride* with a *serial killer* round a *leper colony*.

"It wasn't a *date*!! And it was Cormac! And it was just the graveyard at the back of the house!" I tried *again* to tell her.

Apart from the fact that Cormac, Kennedy and Sonny were only just upstairs and within hearing range, I didn't like to lose my temper anyway (I went a bit red and sweaty, which didn't suit me). But Nonna was *so* maddening!!

It was like this: I'd explained it all about *seventy-five* times to her already while I made her stupid jasmine tea (OK, about six times, but you get the gist). I'd even pointed out REPEATEDLY that Dad was originally supposed to come with us too, which kind of squashed her whole dumb date theory. But did she listen? Nope. Mind you, she was good at listening to Letitia, and clocking on to her Cormac crush. Because of that, she obviously now thought that I – and probably Hannah too – was madly, passionately in love with our trainee undertaker buddy.

As if. . .

"Well, all I'll say *is*," stated Nonna, not backing down, "I'm *very* glad Sonny decided to come along with you as a chaperone!"

"He wasn't a chaperone – he came 'cause he was bored and that was fine, because it WASN'T a *date*!" I said through gritted teeth, feeling my brain practically self-combust with frustration.

"No need to take that tone with me, Sadie! Girls in Spain wouldn't speak to their nonnas like that!"

"That's because girls in Spain don't HAVE nonnas – 'nonna' isn't a Spanish word!!" I exploded.

"Well, whether a word is Spanish or not, it's not the point. The point is that a boy of Cormac's age—"

"Mum!" interrupted Mum, looking sternly at Nonna. "Stop making such a fuss over nothing! It's a simple friendship! "

"Why is everyone getting so annoyed with me?" Nonna responded, acting all innocent. "I mean, if a nonna can't be concerned over the welfare of her grandchild, then I just—"

"Oh, for goodness' sake, BE QUIET for once!"

Wow, listen to that stunned silence. I'd never, *ever* heard my dreamy, ditzy Mum's schoolteacher voice – not even when she must have been driven mad with me and Sonny over the years – but there it was now.

I was rigid with surprise, same as a very startled Nonna, but then the brittle moment was broken by Gran appearing in the doorway with Martha in her arms. She'd heard everything; I could tell by the small smirk playing at the corners of her mouth.

Nonna knew too – I could tell from the way she pursed her lips and narrowed her eyes at Gran.

Yikes, I didn't know what was coming next

(Granny Wars, Part VI-and-a-half?). What I *did* know was that I was planning to get away from here and hide out with the boys as fast as I could. . .

"What's going on?" I asked, walking into my brother's/my temporary room.

I tell you, it was a real relief not to find Sonny, Cormac and Kennedy wedged behind the door, listening in to the ludicrous conversation that had been going on downstairs.

But I hadn't expected to see the three of them on their knees – Sonny between Cormac and Kennedy – peering like three toddlers through the window, the one that faced out on to the pavement and road at the front of the house.

"Kennedy did something *stupid*," Sonny said darkly, without turning round.

"I *said* sorry," Kennedy muttered.

He turned his big, wide face sideways towards Sonny. Don't get me wrong; Kennedy is good-looking (in a big, wide-faced way), and plenty of girls thought he was just *mmm*. They weren't deluded; they just didn't know him like *I* did. If they *knew* him, they'd realize he was more *blahhh* than *mmm*.

"Bit late now," grumbled Sonny, who wasn't the grumbling type.

I stepped over Clyde – who was busily nibbling at Sonny's discarded cycling shorts – and went to check out what they were all so interested in.

"Whoah!!" I muttered, catching a glimpse of Mel the mega-fan, crouched on the pavement outside our house. She was wearing a grey T-shirt, cropped jeans, and . . . uh-oh, had a *white* cardie or hoodie tied round her waist. So she *was* in the graveyard! She'd been my plastic-bag ghost!!

"What's she doing?" I asked, hiding myself behind one of Sonny's Arsenal FC curtains.

"Writing *I love Sadie Rocks!* and *I ♥ Sonny!* in chalk on the pavement and on your garden wall," said Cormac, showing a keen sense of observation.

"But how does she know where you live, Sonny? Or where Dad lives?" I added, thinking about Mel turning up yesterday outside the undertaker's, where the interview was happening up at Kyle and Cormac's place. For that matter, how did she know where Ziggy and Hal and Marcus lived?

"Kennedy told her," growled Sonny.

I frowned down at Kennedy's shamefaced big face. "What? When? And why did you do something so stupid?"

"I didn't tell her *house* numbers!" Kennedy prattled. "I just got talking to her after our first gig at her school and she seemed really nice, and she asked where everyone lived, and I said the areas and then she asked the streets and I told her and she wrote them down, and then I thought it might be a bit weird but I hoped it wasn't. . ."

Kennedy's explanation started big and then fizzled out.

But as he explained and fizzled, it dawned on me that even though Kennedy was big-headed, he was probably still pretty flattered that a fifteen-year-old girl had seemed so interested in talking to him. It made sense. No wonder he'd blabbed so much.

"But hey – she hasn't turned up at *your* house, Kennedy, has she?" I asked, when the thought suddenly struck me.

"No . . . I didn't get round to telling her where I lived 'cause I'd started to think she might be a bit freaky by then," he said uselessly.

"Hey! Look!!"

Cormac alerted us to a sudden flash of red and orange on our front path.

We all looked. The flash of red and orange was Nonna, magnificent as a pirate galleon, stomping towards Mel the mega-fan – with a bucket and mop in her hand.

"Open the window a bit – quick!" I ordered Sonny.

We were still too far away to figure out all of what Nonna was saying to the girl, but we caught the odd phrase. Like "not appropriate" (hey, I'd heard *that* one before), "if your parents knew", "clean this mess up now!" and "promise me—", but we couldn't make out the rest, though we could see Mel sort of nod nervously back at Nonna in response.

"Yay! Go Nonna!!" yelped Sonny, hitting the air as our non-Italian gran took the awkward matter of the stalking girl in hand.

I had to admit it: Nonna was wildly annoying (*tell* me about it), but she had the miracle touch when it came to mad people – possibly because she was quite, quite mad herself.

Wonder how she was at sewing?

That was a *mighty* big hole that Clyde had chewed through Sonny's stage costume. . .

19

Ooh! Guess who?

So what had I learned over the last week or two?

Many, many things, such as:

1) People are complicated, specially when they are called Nonna and have several personalities.
2) You can love people and not like them sometimes (yeah, I'm talking about Nonna again).
3) Never trust an electrical store when they tell you they will "definitely" get the TV cable you need in by the end of the week.
4) Expect eye strain when watching a TV the size of a potato waffle.
5) Cats' tails are flammable and should never be whooshed near a naked flame (e.g., candles).
6) I have cool friends – in comparison to Cormac's non-cool old school buddies – in

the shape of Letty and Hannah (and Cormac), even *with* all the secret rivalries/crushes going on between them.

7) I have a cool family, even if some people in that family aren't directly related to me or each other (hello, Will; hello, Gran).

8) Newspapers will always print the stuff you don't want them to, with headlines you didn't expect like "Teen Tormented By Crazed Stalker" and "Feuding Twins Fuel Future Hit Single". (Gran has already stuck the *Highbury and Islington Gazette* piece in a scrapbook, and ordered extra copies for her old neighbours.)

9) Brothers who annoy you can sometimes turn out to be not so bad (thanks for the loan of half your room, Sonny, even if your socks smell pretty bad), and. . .

10) Twins are definitely *not* psychic, as is commonly thought, otherwise I'd have *known* the big secret that Sonny was keeping from me. . .

"*Nooooo!*" I yelped in horror.

I wasn't yelping at the copy of the *Highbury and Islington Gazette* that Suzanne Hannett was now wafting under my nose. (*Boy*, I hated that photo of me and Sonny sniping at each other – the one that the photographer had taken in Cormac and Kyle's flat when we weren't looking.)

I was yelping at the fact that one of our teachers had just informed us of an unexpected "treat" we'd be having at the end of the day. The whole school was going to the hall to watch a showcase of a young, talented, local band.

No all-sparkling prizes for guessing *who*. . .

And no wonder Sonny had been cagey whenever I'd asked him about how his tour of North London schools was going. He must have known the whole *time* that he'd be appearing at my school.

In front of *me*.

And everyone who *knew* me.

Urgh. . .

"It'll be fine! Remember, no one knows he's your brother!" Letitia whispered to me as we sat in the hall, looking at the as-yet-empty stage.

"Oh, yeah? Well, Suzanne Hannett's been showing *everyone* the newspaper," I muttered blackly.

"OK, so *some* people know he's your brother, but it really will be all right," Letty tried to uselessly reassure me some more.

"HELLO, BOYS AND GIRLS!!"

Help – it was Benny, Mr Cheesily Handsome

195

Band Manager himself, striding on to the stage, booming into a microphone and sounding extra-cheesily perky. All that cheesiness was making me feel a bit nauseous. Or maybe that was just the horror of this gig about to happen in front of me.

Eek . . . and here they came, the five boys, bounding on to the stage behind Benny, in their stupid stage outfits. (At least Sonny was wearing jeans, thanks to Clyde vandalizing his awful neon shorts beyond repair yesterday.)

I willed Sonny to glance around at the audience and find me, so I could demolish him with my Gaze of Death. But he just struck a (stupid) pose and stared straight ahead.

"I'M HERE TODAY FOR A VERY EXCITING REASON," Benny boomed on.

Please don't mention me, please don't mention me, please don't mention me, I prayed silently to any god who might be on duty and listening.

"I'M GOING TO INTRODUCE YOU TO AN AMAZING GROUP OF LOCAL LADS – THE VERY TALENTED . . . SADIE ROCKS!"

OK, he mentioned my name there, but please don't let him explain why the band is called that, I muttered in my head some more, as a few year seven girls squealed in excitement.

Meanwhile, lots of cooler, older boys started

groaning. And no wonder – before they'd even opened their thirteen-year-old mouths, it was glaringly obvious that my brother's group were a junior boy band, aimed straight at little kids, young girls and doting grannies. Cool boys from year eight upwards were *not* their target market. Cool boys from year eight upwards were more likely to use Sadie Rocks as target *practise*.

Speaking of which, a lad's voice from somewhere behind me suddenly grunted out loudly, calling my brother and the rest of the boys a bunch of . . . well, something I'd have to spell out if small children or nervous pets were around to hear.

Had the boys on the stage heard it, and the sniggers that went with it? They sure had. I just saw Sonny *wince* as he tried to hold on to his pose and his dignity.

Hey. . .

Wait a second! Was *this* what he'd been keeping from me? When he'd faked all that "it's going great!"ness about the last week's worth of showcases?

Had Sonny and the boys had to deal with the same mixed reception (i.e., girly squeals and rude gruntings) as this?

You know, I'd bet a million pounds (if I had a million pounds) that they had.

Poor Sonny (and the rest of the boys). Not only did they have a rubbish single to promote, but they were battling against hecklers at the same time. . .

And then – instantly – my sympathy evaporated.

"THIS IS A VERY SPECIAL GIG BECAUSE THE BAND IS NAMED AFTER SONNY – GIVE US A WAVE, SONNY! – AFTER SONNY BIRD'S SISTER, WHO IS A STUDENT HERE!!"

Please, any passing space aliens, I begged to myself, *please beam me up to your spaceship and carry me away from this deep shame. . .*

"Hey, it's all right!" I heard Letty say to me, though her words made absolutely no sense at all. It was absolutely *not* all right that practically everyone in the hall – including teachers – were now staring my way.

"It's *not* all right! The whole school's looking at me!" I hissed back at her, wishing Hannah or Cormac were here to say something marginally more sensible.

"Uh . . . OK. But it's . . . well, it's done now. It can't get any *worse*," said Letty.

Oh, no?

I believe it could. . .

"NOW BEFORE WE PUT OUR HANDS TOGETHER FOR SADIE ROCKS, I'D JUST

LIKE TO SAY THAT IF ANYONE WOULD LIKE TO BUY A T-SHIRT AFTERWARDS, WE LITERALLY *JUST* GOT THE FIRST BATCH IN TODAY. AND A COUPLE OF FANTASTIC LADIES AT THE BACK THERE STEPPED IN TO HELP AT THE LAST MINUTE, AND WILL BE SELLING THEM AFTER THE SHOW!"

What T-shirts? *What* fantastic ladies?

"GIVE US A WAVE, BUNNY AND JOAN, SO EVERYONE KNOWS WHERE YOU ARE!!"

Like in an episode of *Dr Who*, everything felt weird and blurred, as if I'd entered a parallel universe. My head spun in slow-motion, till I fixed on Nonna and Gran, standing at the back of the school hall, grinning excitedly together and wearing – urgh – red T-shirts with "Sadie Rocks!" flashed on the front in some "wacky" white font.

Still, at least no one had to know I was related to these two geriatric promotional girls.

"AND YOU MIGHT LIKE TO KNOW THAT BUNNY AND JOAN ARE SONNY AND SADIE'S GORGEOUS GRANNIES!!"

Great. Lots of giggling faces all round. The only consolation was that Nonna's smile slipped a bit at being called a granny, even if it did have the word gorgeous attached to it.

"You had no idea any of this was going to

happen?" Letitia checked with me, which was dumb but understandable, since the whole thing seemed so surreal.

I mean, two warring grans coming together over badly fitting, naff T-shirts? I guess in the grand scheme of things, I should've been chuffed to witness another truce. But not when it came wrapped in a great big squidgy bundle of shame for *me*.

Uh-oh – Letty was now waving madly at Nonna and Gran, which made them wave madly back at both Letitia and me. I wiggled my fingers half-heartedly.

"Nope. I guess if it was a last minute thing, it happened while I've been here at school today," I mumbled in reply, watching as Nonna mouthed "Surprised?" at me.

"Sadie! Are you . . . *growling*?" Letitia suddenly asked with a frown.

"No!" I lied, clearing my (growling) throat.

"ANYWAY, TIME TO TAKE IT AWAY, BOYS!!!" boomed Benny, now that he'd done his sales pitch and introduced all my insane relatives to the entire world at the same time.

Fantastic. . .

But uh-oh – the shame was now about to start in earnest. Sonny, Kennedy, Marcus, Hal and Ziggy were about to sing their terrible song.

"*Oooooh, oooooh, ooooh, yay-yeah!*" crooned Kennedy, lifting his wide-faced face up to, er, face the crowd.

"*Love is lovely, love is lovely. . .*" the others started harmonizing.

The year seven girls shrieked, just like they were supposed to. All the older boys in the school looked stony-faced in disapproval, but were probably just mulling over suitable jeers for the end of the song. (Though I didn't fancy their chances much if Nonna or Gran heard them. . .)

I glanced behind me, and spotted Nonna and Gran doing . . . well, there were no other words for it but *granny dancing*.

Sigh. Cormac was going to *love* this when I told him.

And here was number eleven in the List of Things That I'd Learned In The Last Week Or Two. . .

11) The Spanish word for embarrassed is *avergonzado*. I looked it up on Sonny's computer at five this morning, when I couldn't sleep, thanks to his – hello! – snoring. I looked it up – along with the Spanish for "annoying" (*molesto*), "boredom" (*tedio*) and "snore" (*ronquido*) because it was the only *tedio*-busting thing I could

think to do at five in the morning, apart from hiding one of every pair of Sonny's socks just to bug him. Anyway, I was currently mucho, *mucho avergonzado*. By my very own *molesto* family members. . .

"Hey, look – Sonny's singing straight *at* you!!" Letty whispered, nudging me hard in the ribs.

So he was.

I gave my twin brother my coolest, most knowing, most sarcastic raised eyebrow in return.

That would show him to keep secrets from me.

Pity it was the wrong eyebrow I'd tried to do it with, in my *avergonzado*'d confusion.

Sonny grinned as he sang, probably trying to stop himself laughing at the sight of his sister in the audience, with the bright red face, deep dark scowl, and one eyebrow boinging up and down like a brown caterpillar on a trampoline.

Number Twelve in the List of Things That I'd Learned In The Last Week Or Two:

12) If provoked, divorce your family.

The end.

(Or *Final*, in Spanish. Or was that Italian. . .?)